BAD RAP

A SERIES INTRODUCING PRIVATE INVESTIGATORS ANGELICA JOY SMITH & BRIANA MARQUEE WATSON

BY REGINA HALE GRADY

Order this book online at www.trafford.com/07-0504
or email orders@trafford.com

Most Trafford titles are also available at major online book retailers.

Note for Librarians: A cataloguing record for this book is available from Library and Archives Canada at www.collectionscanada.ca/amicus/index-e.html

ISBN: 978-1-4251-2100-6

We at Trafford believe that it is the responsibility of us all, as both individuals and corporations, to make choices that are environmentally and socially sound. You, in turn, are supporting this responsible conduct each time you purchase a Trafford book, or make use of our publishing services. To find out how you are helping, please visit www.trafford.com/responsiblepublishing.html

Our mission is to efficiently provide the world's finest, most comprehensive book publishing service, enabling every author to experience success. To find out how to publish your book, your way, and have it available worldwide, visit us online at www.trafford.com/10510

www.trafford.com

North America & international
toll-free: 1 888 232 4444 (USA & Canada)
phone: 250 383 6864 ♦ fax: 250 383 6804
email: info@trafford.com

The United Kingdom & Europe
phone: +44 (0)1865 722 113 ♦ local rate: 0845 230 9601
facsimile: +44 (0)1865 722 868 ♦ email: info.uk@trafford.com

10 9 8 7 6 5 4

In Loving Memory

Reverend Glaskor Douglas, Bertha Lee Douglas, W. Henry Hale, Loretta Douglas Hale, Lugenia Gantt, Francis E. Grady, Ethel Grady, Gladys Samuels and Kevin Douglas.

Rest in Eternal Peace

1

I guess it's a good thing to have friends in high places or maybe you're just sucking the right dick. Because obtaining prime real estate on Queens Boulevard these days is no small feat. Angelica Joy Smith wonders this to herself one sunny September morning while driving her metallic gray Mazda Millennia into the parking garage of the newly constructed white superstructure in Kew Gardens, Queens.

The smell in the air in September is refreshing. School is starting and the kids are so vibrant, for now. They are freshly bathed and sporting new hairstyles, new outfits, new backpacks which contain crisp loose-leaf paper of which makes all contribute to what makes September so invigorating. Angelica Joy Smith relishes in this belief.

Angelica's partner and best friend "Beamer" (yes, the supermodel, girlfriend keeps it real) operates Smith and Watson Private Investigations at 8700 Queens Boulevard, Suite 1109, Kew Gardens, NY.

Kew Gardens in the 1800's was once a wooded area known as "Hay's Town" until it attracted the attention of landscape architect Edward Richmond and developer Albon P. Man. Together they purchased a tract of land extending north along Jamaica Plank Road to

Union Turnpike, and named it Richmond Hill, after a famous point near London. By the turn of the century, Man's sons Artur and Alrick, had subdivided the most desirable Northernpiece in the north. They called their community Kew Gardens because its beauty reminded them of the Royal Botanical Gardens at Kew in England. By 1921, the Man brothers built in excess of 300 English and Colonial style homes, pushing to make Kew Gardens both unique and attractive. The area was once so exclusive it advertised itself as being "restricted", with homebuyers being selected by the Kew Gardens Corporation, which allowed only those who were considered prominent and desirable to live there. Dr. Ralph Bunche, a black man was one of Kew Garden's most noted residents.

Today Kew Gardens is filled with a mix of private homes, high-rise condominiums, offices and shops. It's also the site of both the Queens Borough Hall and Queens Criminal Courts, lawyers and related businesses have offices within the area, especially along Queens Boulevard. It's a big deal for two African American women to be conducting a thriving business in Kew Gardens so they do all they can to represent.

Beamer and Angelica have been "girls" since the eighth grade. Beamer's family moved across the street from A.J.'s in Queens and

A.J. was forced to befriend the nerdy new girl when Bianca's little brother was killed by a drunk driver. A.J.'s mom had witnessed the accident and ran to get Beamer's mother who was inconsolable. Their families have been connected ever since. It also didn't hurt that Beamer had one of the best doll collections that A.J. had ever seen. Beamers Uncle Smitty traveled a lot and he always brought her a doll from wherever he went. A.J. holds a degree in Criminal Justice and was once a New York City Police Detective. Beamer was discovered by a photographer Paris-based photographer when her Uncle Smitty took her as a high school graduation gift. Beamer became a world famous supermodel.

Here's the Daily News as opposed to the Sunday New York Times version of how a former New City Police Detective and a Supermodel became enjoined as Private Investigators: Brianna's "Uncle Smitty", Lawrence Smith a retired NY Police Detective and owner of Watson Private Investigations Agency was found dead from an alleged suicide. He was found hanging in his garage among his cherished black art collection. Beamer refused to believe her favorite uncle, who always told her to live life to the fullest had killed himself.

So, when she asked A.J. to look into the case on the down low A.J. had to, it killed her to see her best friend so distraught. Besides, Uncle Smitty also had been just as much an uncle to A.J. Uncle Smitty never married and Beamer inherited his Private Investigation agency and insisted on assisting with proving her Uncle's death was in fact a murder. Apparently a piece of art Uncle Smitty purchased in Africa had belonged to a sacred tribe which insisted on having it back. Uncle Smitty wanted to recoup some of the money his spent on the relic; but the tribe, however, would not hear of it and things got ugly. Proving it was murder nearly cost them their lives, too; it did, however, cost A.J. her job and made headlines.

The media called them a modern day Cagney and Lacey. They thought the comparison was hilarious. Their idols are Shaft, Cleopatra Jones and Bugs Bunny. A.J. is 5'4" with bushy black hair with a gray curl she affectionately calls her personality. She constantly wears high heels and designer suits. Beamer is a black Dominican, 6' and has an unruly mop of light brown curly hair. She always wears black. After they solved Uncle Smitty's murder Beamer retired from modeling and suggested they run the agency. A.J. had nothing else to lose. She actually thought she would be humoring Beamer; after all one would take them seriously, especially not Uncle Smitty's former employees who had laughed when they were told them the plan. A Supermodel and an ex-cop, private eyes, and women no-less, they had them doomed from the beginning.

Insulted Beamer had set out to prove her brains matched her beauty. Beamer through her connections had taken a crash course at Hick Harris's Private Detective Academy in Los Angeles. Beamer had earned a black belt in karate. She is an amateur photographer (a long standing hobby). She can pick any lock and she actually studies different locks and alarms systems. She regularly practices surveillance techniques as a side hobby. A.J. had been busy was trying to make sense of Uncle Smitty's filing system, as well as reviewing his pending cases. Three years has passed during which Beamer and A.J. have demonstrated extreme professionalism and have built a reputation for conducting business with the utmost discretion. They have a client list that would knock most skeptics on their collective asses.

They've provided services in several high profile headline grabbing cases and have been featured in numerous magazines namely, Essence, Heart and Soul, Sister to Sister Magazines and their personal favorite Gun Magazine. A.J.'s law enforcement contacts and Beamers entertainment connections have kept them busier than they could imagine. They relocated from

Brooklyn to Kew Gardens and renamed the agency Smith and Watson Private Investigations specializing in Missing Persons, Employment Screening, Background/Personal History, Discreet Photos, Physical and Electronic Surveillance, Body guarding/Escorting and Pre-marital background checks.

A.J. waited for the garage attendant Jose to lift the electronic arm and thereafter drove to the second level where she parked in one of their five reserved spots. A.J. did a little car dancing to Slave's Just a Touch of Love put the car in park and cut the engine. Then she carefully opened the door so as to not catch her stocking, something she had a bad habit of doing. She smoothed the skirt of her gray Calvin Klein suit and got her James Bond steel briefcase from the passenger seat. A.J. and Beamer both have identical James Bond kits provided to them by their technical wizard, Joseph Woo and yes, ladies, he is all that. The cases contain a small tool kit, lock pick kit, Swiss army knife, metal detector, binoculars, shades (four no less), wigs (2), a 120-zoom camera, another throw away cell phone and a change of underwear; no explanation needed nor offered to anyone, some things a girl just does not reveal.

It's about 7:30 a.m. and her high-heeled footsteps play loudly on the concrete floor. A.J. takes the elevator to the lobby and greets Rollo the guard on reception duty. Their offices are on the 15th floor and, again, she wonders how Beamer was able to acquire the space; apparently another of her "friends". A.J. stopped asking Beamer about her friends and the favors they bestow upon her, so long as Beamer states criminal wrong doing is not an issue.

Upon entering the bank of elevators leading to their office suite A.J. silently thanks the good lord for their blessings, some days their good fortune overwhelms her, but it's all good. The elevator stops on 15, the doors open and she exits. Immediately she is overwhelmed by a foul smell. She then slows her pace and draws her gun from her suit's rear waist ban. Her temperature rises as a thin film of perspiration covers her back. She licks her lips as if to cool herself. Her heart raced which brings a sadistic grin to her face. She is always aware of how busy the devil is and it amuses her that she has the ability to recognize him in what ever form he appears. This "sixth sense", depending on what situation she's trying to get out off or into, has been a blessing. Usually when she smells this particular odor something sinister is up. It's not as rancid as the smell of death but can best be described as being a mixture of rotten fish, burning tar, and a subway toilet. At times it's been so strong it has caused her to gag. When alone she would ask the people around her: "Do you smell that?", often they would reply, "Smell what?" Beamer calls it her "Spidey Sense Tingling."

As she approached their office just around a short hallway the smell got stronger. The cleaning lady observes the drawn gun drops her mop and runs. She slowly lowers her weapon and peeks around the corner only to spot a gift wrapped box. She observes the box is addressed to her. The box has bright floral print and it sits on the floor in front of her office door. She starts to gag. Beamer had one of those old glass window doors made, doors like you see in those old Private Dick movies. The glass was etched with the name Smith & Watson Private Investigations and their logo, a small pair of binoculars, a magnifying glass, a gun and a pair of a shapely woman's crossed legs each separately placed in a crosshair.

She recovered quickly; knelt, opened her briefcase and extracted the hand held metal detector. She ran it over the box. She got no unusual beeps and mouthed "Thank You Jesus", picked up the box and stepped into the reception area. She placed the box on the reception desk, put away her keys, and proceeded to open the box.

Shenequa the receptionist and Angelica's niece, had so many pictures of her baby on the desktop she almost couldn't find space to operate. A.J. almost fainted when she lifted the tissue paper and saw a stuffed clown!!!! She felt her entire body go hot. She thought this is somebody's idea of a bad joke and, she began to plan how she's going to hurt them. Only a few people and now you know how she feels about clowns. Actually, she hates clowns. Her aversion to clowns comes from an incident she experienced while at a red light in Little Neck, Queens. While returning from Worth Repeating, a consignment shop in Locust Valley, Long Island a car pulled up next to her and a yell heard was accompanied by the toot of a car horn. The car's driver was heard to say "Could you tell me how to get to Union Turnpike?" She looked to her left and saw a man in full clown regalia. She completely froze; mouth agape and all she could imagine was, what an ingenious way to rob/rape/attack someone.

She could see it now -

Police Officer: "Maam could you describe who did this to you?"

A.J.: "It was BOZO!!!!"

She couldn't respond. Her voice was lost and the light must have changed because Bozo yelled "Asshole!" and sped off. As she sat there agape and staring after his car traffic stalled behind her and car horns blared. She had to pull over to collect herself. After that, the thought of Stephen King's evil movie "IT", the movie "Killer Clowns from Outer Space" and the John Wayne Gacy Story, has occupied her thoughts that those people, pretending to spread joy, are probably on the FBI's Most Wanted List. Now, no one should get offended and don't organize 100 clowns to set up protest outside their office but - THIS IS PERSONAL!!!! This could evoke a 'terminator' mentality and cause a breakdown.

She left the box on Shenequa's desk and unlocked their office door. She looked over her shoulder at the box as if the "thing" would jump out of the box. She needed some space between herself and that thing. She sat down in the dimly sun lit office; suddenly her cell phone rang startling the living daylights out of her. It was Beamer.

Beamer: "Smith!!" She yelled.

A.J. usually yells back: "Watson!!"

"I hope you don't think your little gift is funny," she said.

"What gift? I love you but, it's so not that serious" Beamer said.

"You know I do not enjoying bullshittin' around before I've eaten my breakfast", said

A.J. (non joking tone).

"What are you talking about, girl?" Beamer replied.

"There was a boxed gift, wrapped and addressed to me left in front of our office door this morning and, it's a freakin CLOWN!!!!"A.J. shouted."

"And you think that I sent you a clown?" (Realizing how upset her girlfriend sounded). "Don't trip, every time I see one now, Thanks to you, I get the willies thinking it's a pervert in disguise."

"Just get here okay!!" A.J. disconnects the call.

Then she was suddenly startled again by the piped in sounds of Frank Sinatra crooning "Luck be a Lady Tonight". Shenequa, is straight up ghetto but loves Sinatra, go figure. Pray for her. Excited Shenequa burst into the office holding the box and exclaimed, "Is this for me?" Not waiting for an answer, as usual, she runs on: "He's so cute. I love clowns" - she stopped and with a look of concern she continued talking but slowly and said "Why are you sitting in the dark?"

A.J. stood up and pointed to the door. She was about to loose it when Beamer walked in, took the clown, and stuffed it in the box. She gave Shenequa the box and ushered her out of the office telling her to "GET RID OF IT

NOW!!!!" AND HOLD ALL OUR CALLS !!" Beamer closed the door in Shenequa's confused face.

2

When Briana pulled over her bike (a Harley-Davidson) to answer her vibrating cell phone and saw it was a call from A.J., she immediately knew something wasn't right. A.J. and Beamer have been best friends almost 15 years and have each others back no matter what. A.J. never has calls in the morning unless something is up. A.J. handles the majority of the business administration while they both handle the investigative aspects. Beamer gets claustrophobic when cooped up to long. A.J. often calls her Hawk (from Spenser for Hire) which she doesn't mind because he's her idol; she emulates his all black get-ups and the way he "keeps his tricks in line". He knows the power of his dick and she knows the power of her pussy. Her dream is to be like Hawk, John Shaft, and Cleopatra Jones - ass kicking and sexy as hell.

When she got to the building she parked her bike where she wanted. Mo-fo's must be living on Mars or smoking some new shit if they dared to mess with her ride. She pulled off her helmet, unlatched her Bat case and fluffed her naturally curly hair and proceeded to enter the office building. Beamer, 6', a size 8 and toned from working out, captured attention on and off her ride, this is not out of the ordinary.

When she got to the building, Rollo, the security guard was on duty. "Whoo !! Wee !!!, Good Morning Midnight!" Rollo said in his thick southern drawl. She leaned over the desk and ran her index finger from his collarbone down to his belly and softly pokes him.

"You been a good boy Rollo?" she asked in almost a whisper.

"Yes Maam, you know I ain't misbehaven."

"Who's the boss?" Beamer asked. Running her tongue over her lips and showing some cleavage, and intensifying his gaze.

When he caught his breath he swallowed and a bead of sweat formed on his brow. He said "You know you the boss Miss Midnight."

"Good boy", she touched his cheek and said now tell Mama who worked this desk last night?"

"Brucey worked the 12 a.m. til 8 a.m. Maam" he said.

"Now see how easy that was, me leading," pausing to touch his lips, "you following?"

"I could love you so good" he said. He looked up at her in full sweat.

"When I'm ready for you, you'll know" she said and walked away in her bad ass effortless runway strut. She got into the elevator, turned around and held his stare until the door closed. "Sufferin Succotash" Beamer said through her teeth. And aloud she said "Lord forgive me, but I just can't help it, he's makes it too easy."

When she entered the reception area and saw the box. She examined it briefly, and looked up to see Shenequa holding the clown up to A.J. who was about to leap over her desk. A.J.'s usual morning routine, since she arrived the earliest, was opening the blinds, turning on the computers, checking late night messages and starting the water for tea had not been done. Beamer knew A.J. was outdone. Beamer put Shenequa out. She then went around the desk to A.J., who now had her head in her hands and put her hand on A.J.'s arm. Beamer asked, "Are you okay?"

"Yeah just a little startled." A.J. said exhaling. "Ain't nobody but that old devil trying to steal my glory."

"Girl you know he always trying to stir up shit to make it stink when you're feeling too good about life and the Lord," Briana says.

"We're just too happy for him, hater." Replies A.J.

A.J. and Beamer were raised in the Baptist Church and do not profess to be any type of holy rollers. But they do believe he is in control of all things. They are at a point in their lives where they refuse to let anything or anyone steal their glory. They focus on the things that really matter in this one life we are blessed with. A.J. is always saying "Have no regrets, this is life with its ups and downs, pray for more ups". Beamer's motto is "This is not a dress rehearsal."

"You want some tea?" Bianca asks.

"Yes thanks, with a smile on her face, "You know it never fails, whenever I am feeling truly thankful for my blessings here comes the devil. I was just in my car thanking the good Lord", A.J. said shaking her head.

Beamer busied herself with making the tea.

"You want me to check out where that box may have come from?" Beamer asks. Gesturing with her head towards the reception area A.J. said "No, it's probably just some asshole and you know I have zero tolerance for those" A.J. said shaking her head and still smiling.

"Who would know that you don't like clowns? Beamer asked. "That shit is personal."

Making a face A.J. said, "Beamer, you know how we run our mouths I could have said it and someone overheard it. We joke about it, but I'm serious about it, if I have to, I will hurt a clown." A.J. said shaking her fist like an eighth grader.

"Well as for as us running our mouths, yeah, you do talk to much girl" Beamer replies with a smile.

A.J. looks amusingly offended and clutches her bosom. Beamer walked over to her desk and placed the tea in front of her and says "As for that little gift, to quote Mr. Fudd "Be very very afraid."

Taking a sip of tea and closing her eyes A.J. let out a small sigh and says, "Thanks, doll." Then in a soft voice says, "Beamer?"

Beamer turns to see what A.J. wants detecting a bit of trepidation but ready to help her best friend.

"Yes?"

A.J. has her head down and slowly looks up; smiles at Beamer and says, "You do talk too much." They both laugh. Beamer says, "I'll get things started here, you just sit tight" while placing a hand on A.J.'s shoulder. She then proceeded around the office opening blinds, turning on the computers, checking her in mail box, watering Benny our plant, sorting through A.J.'s incoming mail box and checking the Bat phone for informant messages.

Their office space was designed by a now prominent former working girl, Caramela Brown. Brown was a former working girl whom A.J. once let her hid out in her old apartment from her pimp. A.J. came home to find her apartment totally rearranged, paint, drapes and the works. A.J. offered her the space on the following conditions: that she volunteer at Dress for Success, an organization that helps low income women get suited up for work; (an organization very near to A.J.'s heart)and, that Caramela enroll in a design school. Now, girlfriend is one of the most sought after interior decorators around. Unfortunately she had to come out about her past due to a big mouth former client who was down on his luck and ready to "out" her. But, you can't keep a strong sister down. Brown is now an advocate and role model for women in the 'life'.

The decor of Smith and Watson Investigative offices exhibited a comfortable confidence without being to homely. An entire wall is lined with bookcases. The oversized dark mahogany L-shaped desk and file cabinets are made of a lighter mahogany; the carpet consists of olive, rust and brown earth tones. Their plush leather swivel chairs are rust colored while the blinds are made of chamois colored baby pine.

"What's on the calendar?" A.J. asks. "You finish tailing the Montgomery husband?"

"Yeah," Beamer said with a sigh shaking her head.

"Another woman?"

Beamer makes a face.

"A man?" A.J. said.

"No, after work Mr. Charles Montgomery III goes to the "hood" to a bodega on DeKalb Avenue, Brooklyn and plays the Joker Poker machine."

"Whew, that's a relief. We don't have to report yet another case of adultery or another brother on the down low."

"He spends at least 3 hours after work there and he seems to be having a ball. It's when he's heading home that he looks absolutely sick."

"Is he winning anything at least?"

"Are you kidding?, In the hood! Honey-child they got that fish on the hook. They're serving drinks and fish on Friday for goodness sakes!!"

A.J. presses her intercom, "Shenequa, she said, could you make sure the team is reminded about the scheduled meeting this Thursday?"

"I sent an e-mail to everyone, but no problem, I'll request confirmations."

"Thank you" A.J. said as she sits back and finally exhales.

3

THE EPISODE

CASE #1374 (THE BAD RAPPER)

"We have an appointment with that Phenom character this morning, Jesus, what a ridiculous name. She shivers. I can't stand saying it."

"He's coming here; you talked to him?" Jumping up, she points to the floor.

"He left a message on my business cell very late yesterday. The message said the Donald referred him."

"I called him back and told him it was disrespectful to call after 11:00 pm and only because of Donald I would see him first thing this morning."

I've seen him at some industry parties but I never met him."

"You mean you haven't? I thought you knew all of those people."

"We sometimes run in the same circles but, unless my bird is making bubbles and chirping so badly for his worm, I approach no man. Besides, now don't get me wrong cause I ain't mad at no thug, but he seems a little impressed with himself. And that turns me off."

"Well", A.J. said while she looked at her Anne Klein silver chain link watch, "he should be here soon."

All of a sudden Shenequa is screaming -

Beamer leaps over her desk; A.J. somehow gets around hers and they both draw their guns. They carry the Smith & Wesson, model 3913, stainless steel, polymer grip, single stack (7 shot clip with one in the pipe) small recessed hammer type semi-automatic pistols. They both carried them in a back pancake holster. Beamer had looked at A.J. and nodded; Shenequa continued to scream as A.J. pulled open the door. Beamer was first through the door with A.J. on her heels. And then they realized what the commotion was all about.

Shenequa seeing them with their guns drawn caused her to scream at them. Beamer and A.J. looked at each other and put their guns away. A.J. placed her hands on her hips and gave Shenequa 'the look'. Because, if it's the last thing she does it will have been to teach that child some class.

Phenom was standing there with his hands up looking every bit the child, A.J. remembered. Shenequa managed to catch the look, she stopped screaming and lowered her head. Beamer and A.J. holstered their guns and apologized for the reception, A.J. opened the office for him to enter. Beamer followed and so does Shenequa who beamed from ear to ear, Beamer turned and gave her a look that stopped her in her tracks. Beamer instructed her to hold their calls and closed the door in

Shenequas dejected face.

"Please have a seat" A.J. said, as she and Beamer took theirs. "Again we apologize for the reception."

"That's awright - she's a fan" Phenom says.

"She has a lot to learn A.J. said. "This is my partner Briana Watson."

Beamer nodded her head but also picks up on A.J.'s tone and let's her lead.

Phenom gave Beamer a sideways glance and slyly lifted his chin in a ghetto gesture making no movement to shake her hand.

What a gentleman, A.J. thought.

"Look like yaw'll are doing awright", Phenom said as he looked around the office.

"This is the result of extremely hard work not just a few referrals. We've worked extremely hard to make this company one of the most discreet and reputable investigative agencies in the city", A.J. said with complete attitude.

Beamer again gave A.J. that look Bugs Bunny gets when his entire head turns into a question mark; wondering where her rudeness is coming from.

Phenom is one of those new young rapper's turned entrepreneur. They think because they've been accepted into Entertainment society they are a success. When "we" actually know most of them got their start-up money from hustling. Their critics suspect their source of wealth or financial backing came from questionable sources but can't prove it. Hosting charity events, giving out computers, holding book drives for needy children in the projects, giving out turkeys at Thanksgiving and holding hip-hop celebrity basketball tournaments to me is all good, but in no way does it make you a member of the elite. Because we all know for most of them you can take the ghetto out of the boy.... These things in their minds probably exonerate them from their past indiscretions.

He was part of a youth group that A.J. counseled as community service in the Gray Lane projects while she was attending college. She tried to reach out to him but he didn't want to be "rescued", as he put it, and chose the hustlers life.

He gave A.J, an especially hard time since she no longer lived in the hood. According to him, she thought she was better than the people living in Gray Lane. A.J. suspected he was behind many of the entertainment referrals they got requesting escorts, body guard services and background checks for several of his hit-makers and employees of his record label, Phenomenal Records. Many of the invitations they received to big celebrity events were suspect to her but, she couldn't be sure because of Beamers connections and she was not going to put that much energy into looking into it. Beamer was completely committed to having a world renowned organization and stand on their reputation.

Beamer and A.J. started "Uplift Your Life", a program for the parents and youth in Gray Lane. Phenom's record label donated fifteen computers to their after school program for which they also got several lawyers, police officers, correction officers and other private investigators to volunteer their time. A.J. would have refused the donation but the members of the board were so excited and impressed that A.J. was big enough to keep her personal feelings about him to herself.

He seemed to be trying to say "Hey, look at me I'm legitimate, I belong. Other than news coverage A.J. hadn't seen him face to face in many years. He couldn't even look her straight in the eye. This person who appeared to be grandstanding for the media and all of America was still intimidated by A.J.

Beamer says most people are intimidated by A.J. but couldn't fathom why. According to A.J., she is a 'puddy tat'. It's been reported that Phenom is now worth several million dollars; owns a home in the Hamptons (ha! We bet the neighbors love that); a brownstone in Park Slope, Brooklyn and, a condo in Manhattan where his office is located. He's about 6', with a medium chocolate complexion, about a quarter of an inch of hair and handsome in a GQ model kind of way (if you like that type). His steel blue double-breasted suit looks like one of the new FUBU suits they saw during Fashion Week with a 1950's style cut, a fob watch was dangling from a platinum chain, a very classy touch. He is the CEO and Founder of Project Records and just recently launched Phenomenal Indie Films. He also has seven kids and three "baby-mamas". He's single. Limps but walks with a cane due to a gun shot wound and has the annoying habit of constantly saying: "You know what I'm saying."

"Must be really important you coming here in person" A.J. said, with a sarcastic tone in her voice, twirling a Parker writing pen.

"I know my label does a lot of business with your company, you know what I'm saying" he said "and I ..

"No", A.J. said, in an annoyed tone interrupting him. "We don't know what you're saying. Our firm appreciates all the business we get but we are not interested in publicity nor are we indebted to anyone. We have a reputation for keeping confidences and operating with complete discretion."

"Look I didn't come here to get into anything with you, you know what I'm saying he said and sighed an annoyed breath. "I need to utilize your services". He glanced at Beamer and leaned towards A.J.'s desk and said, "Could we talk in private?" He looked back at Beamer and caught the look she gave him. He tried to recover by saying "No offense."

"None taken" Beamer said sweetly but doesn't move.

"Ms. Watson and I are business partners and keep no secrets when it comes to our clients, unless you are a close and personal friend, which you aren't" A.J. said. "This business can be very dangerous if we don't watch each others back. Is that a problem for you?"

"Naw, Naw, I hear that, I hear that" he repeated and of course he followed it up with a good old "you know what I'm sayin". "Someone is trying to blackmail me", he said as he looked down at the floor. For a minute he looked embarrassed. But, when he lifted his head a dangerous rage which reminds A.J. of the angry little boy he used to be.

"Blackmailed how?" A.J. asks.

"I received a package in the mail, of a disc" he paused to fix his tie, obviously uncomfortable.

"When was this?" A.J. asked as she and Beamer started taking notes. Shenequa finds this time appropriate to start the office music and Linda Clifford's "Runaway Love" comes on.

Beamer and A.J. give each other a look and A.J. shakes her head.

"About two weeks ago, I been tripping since then and practically vacated my Manhattan place in order to think, Dee, I mean Donald suggested that I call you."

"Was there a note? Beamer asks. If so did you keep the original packaging?"

"Naw, I ripped up the packaging but I have the note" G.L. said clinching his fist.

"Where exactly was it mailed to?" asks Beamer.

"My place in Manhattan; it came by courier, I've been in Connecticut trying to figure out what to do."

"Let me guess this tape is x-rated" A.J. says sounding bored.

"I'm not in it" Phenom says defensively and looks at A.J. defiantly.

"Then who is?"

Phenom blows out his breath and shakes his head and mumbles "My sister."

A.J. quickly said "Speak up" as if talking to a naughty child, tapping her pen on her desk.

Beamer shot her a look.

Phenom clears his throat and said "It's a tape of my sister, her best friend Larissa and Ducal Davis."

Ducal "The Double Dee" Davis was a good

friend of Phenom and the press gave the baller flack for hanging out with a former alleged drug dealer. Not to mention Ducal's team mate and best friend Keyshawn Strong who was banned from the league for not adhering to the collective bargaining rule "three strike drug rule". But Davis defended Phenom telling the media that Phenom had watched out for him in the parks and had kept him out of trouble.

"The baller Ducal Davis?" A.J. asks. She and Beamer are avid sports fans and share Knicks and Nets season tickets.

"The one who died with his entire family in that plane crash last year?"

The Davis Ducal "The Double Dee" had invested in a private jet company; he was a well trained pilot. Unfortunately, last year he got caught in a terrible snow storm trying to surprise his family with a ski trip to Denver for Christmas.

"Well this person obviously wants something from you since they can't get it from Davis. He doesn't have any heirs or family left to extort."

Beamer sat up "Where in Connecticut are you staying?"

"New London, I go there to write" Phenom says proudly.

Beamer's thinking "O.K. this is where my Bugs Bunny ear reaches down to scratch my head," A.J. rolls her eyes thinking there goes the neighborhood.

A.J. and Beamer spend a lot of time in Mystic, Connecticut which is the next town from New London, where they recently purchased waterfront property.

Phenom pulls a sheet of paper out of his suit jacket.

"That the note?" A.J. asks. A.J. takes out a plastic envelop and the shakes the letter open. Holding it by the corner of its page careful not spread her prints and inserts it into the envelope sealing the top.

YOU KNOW WHAT THIS MEANS SLICK. WE WILL BE IN TOUCH ABOUT THE WHEN AND WHERE TO BRING THE MONEY.

"Have you told your sister about this?" A.J. asked.

"Naw, Phenom says looking down, twisting his hands, I should protect her. She's very street smart but, I didn't get her out of that life to have her dragged down again. I want to kill this."

"Whoa" Beamer says, holding up her hands.

A.J. sits up in her chair and says forcefully, "Kill, we don't accept cases so that our clients can exact revenge."

"I'm sorry, Phenom says collecting himself. I'm just not used to being this helpless. I'm a business man, a black man and need to conduct myself as such."

"Amen" Beamer says as A.J. shoots her a look.

"I remember someone once saying that we are a proud people and shouldn't give others a reason to sit around the dinner table and talk about us, that we see enough bad news on TV."

A.J. stared at him and recalled the speech she gave a group of boys who were fighting at the Youth Center. She thought Russell had walked out but, she later noticed him watching from the doorway.

"But you're on the news all the time …"A.J. says her voice softening. First Choice's "Dr. Love" starts to play and Beamer is doing everything she can to keep from chair dancing.

"Yeah promoting my company, and charity events but, I try not to embarrass myself or my people. I know when I first started I was a bit obnoxious but what young kid from the ghetto wouldn't be."

Beamer looked at A.J. and knew that was one of A.J.'s favorite lines; something was going on and she wasn't in on it.

A.J. let a little smile escape as she nodded her head approvingly, but quickly snapped back into business mode.

"Have you watched the tape in its entirety?" she asked.

"Naw, I saw enough."

"We would need to question them both, one or both of them would know who shot it."

"Better you than me, but I would like to be there when you tell them."

"That's not our job." Beamer says

"Look I'll pay you. I just can't tell her this." Phenom says while looking down.

"If we take the case, we'll have to talk to her, we'll call you in a day or so to let you know if we can take this on." A.J. said in a stern voice.

Beamer cuts her a look knowing she is busting his balls.

"A day or so, what if I hear from these people today? I need to know what I'm going to do now, not in a few days." Phenom says.

"O.K., leave a number where you can be reached and we'll call you by close of business today" Beamer says.

"No problem, he said exaggeratingly, you know what I'm sayin."

A.J. rolls her eyes. "Just be clear that once we accept an assignment we usually like to finish it. Our clients sometimes get their undies in a bunch when we start rattling the bones in their closets and they can't handle the "so called" invasion of privacy. We may uncover something that you may not be happy with and we will not be part of anything criminal."

As Phenom got up to leave he looks around awkwardly realizing that he has been dismissed.

"Nice to have finally met you" he said to Beamer.

"The pleasure is mine, sir" Beamer says in a playful southern belle voice.

"Bye" he says to A.J. and leaves.

A.J. just nods and walks him to the door and closed it. A.J. then reopens it to catch Shenequa covering her mouth and shivering. Shenequa spots A.J. and tried to compose herself. When Ghetto Lord is safely out of earshot A.J. said to Shenequa "Not one word to anyone that he was here."

"You know I wouldn't do that Auntie", Shenequa says in a hurtful tone.

A.J. gave her a nod; and closed the door and takes a seat at her desk.

"Okay Talk!" Beamer says as she leaned on her desk and bopping her head to the beat of the music. "I know you feel like someone pissed in your cornflakes this morning but that's no excuse for being rude to a client and a famous one at that!"

"Famous!" A.J. said as she blows her breath, sniffs and asked "Do you smell something?" looking around suspiciously.

"You're still tripping from this morning".

"It was probably that damn boy" A.J. says giving her goofy beady eye look.

"Talk!!!" Beamer shouts.

A.J. then proceeds to tell Beamer how she knew Phenom.

"Damn!" "I heard he had it rough growing up and you knew him and never said anything? And what was that about the clients we get?"

"They were assignments we couldn't refuse. At first I thought they were publicity from Uncles murder and then one of our clients mentioned his name. I realized we were working with that punk. Besides tracking your high society friends, runaway kids and following their wives and husbands was getting a little boring."

"At first I didn't even put it together. I always dealt with Mamie in regards to providing personal security. But I thought she ran her own agency then she mentioned going to her bosses birthday party. I put two and two together and came up with a knucklehead. I decided I could be a bigger person and wouldn't have to deal directly with him. You know I would never compromise our friendship or our reputation to get business. I'd just put all my girls back on the streets, Bambi."

They both shared a laugh remembering how A.J. used to have pet names for their small but tight crew, Beamer was Bambi, Rhonda was Candy, Celia was Champagne and A.J. was the Madame.

"What else is on for today?" Beamer asks as she goes over to her desk and sits. You sure you are O.K.?"

"Yeah, I'm actually feeling a little ghetto now, I could kick some ass. She says jumping up moving into a karate pose, "Maybe I should go work on my golf stroke."

"Maybe you need to get stroked." Beamer said.

"What I need to do is call up NASA and find out when the next space shuttle is leaving because you earthlings have worked my last nerve. And I will get balled when I need to" A.J. said and gave Beamer the finger.

They both stuck out their tongues at one another and roll their eyes exaggeratedly.

Their computer monitors have their company emblem on their screens.

"Mrs. Harver referred her girlfriend to

us. Mrs. Harver's husband was fooling around with the babysitter in the jungle gym in their back yard. She had tried to set up a video camera herself but couldn't catch him in the act. Joseph Woo, our technical advisor and gadget specialist set up indoor and outdoor cameras and nailed them on his first try. "And Dale Cunningham lost his witness Lucky, again. Did you know that?" Beamer asked.

"No, he beeped me over the weekend but I just thought he wanted some phone" A.J. said.

"I can't believe that nice man likes phone sex or that a nice girl like you gives it."

"Hey, we all have our thing. He likes it from me!" A.J. says as she breathes on her short well manicured nail and polishes them on her suit. "But it's so dead for me. It's like something once you discovered you can do it so easily you lose interest in it. I love being his friend but I'm going to have to tell him fall back on that."

"You done turned somebody's nice boy into a phone head."

The ladies finish checking their E-Mail in silence.

"I'll get back to Dale before he gets himself killed" A.J. says.

"Let's just hope Lucky's luck hasn't run out" Beamer says quickly.

"Mammie Balding needs security services at

a Listening Party for Monei on the 28th".

"I got this one" Beamer says.

"Groupie!" A.J. says.

"Hey all work and no play makes me horny. Besides, I got a new outfit."

"Black of course."

"As my ass."

"Yellow heifer!"

Before they can get into their behind closed doors banter Shenequa buzzes Beamer - Beamer's speaker chirps.

"Yes", Beamer says.

"Um, that judge friend of yours" - Shenequa clears her throat and says - "Judge Murphy called and he said it's urgent that you get back to him."

Beamer smiles at A.J. noting Shenequa's effort "Thank you, Shenequa."

"You're welcome."

"Ah, Sugar Daddy needs his fix."

"It's not like that and you know it." Beamer says defensively.

"Maybe for you but not for him; you know what Chris Rock said, "They don't want to be your friend, they want to fuck you."

"He could be my daddy."

"Just like I said, besides he's so fine I don't know how you haven't yet, I just hope when you do you'll tell me how it was."

"You know you always talking about I got

issues but you are a stone cold freak."

A.J. dramatically puts her hands on her breast and in her southern accent says "Why maam you offend my honor."

"Excuse me, there is no honor among working girls."

"Hey, watch your mouth" A.J. said as she got up and walked towards their private bathroom.

Beamer picked up the phone and called Michael on his private line.

4

The Honorable Judge Michael Murphy was the widowed son of a noted black New York City Defense lawyer who married a bi-racial renowned painter who had no shame about passing for white. Michael suffered through a strained relationship with his mother. He was as dark as his Grandfather whom his mother despised and rarely saw since her nervous breakdown two year earlier. Beamer met Michael at A.J.'s thirtieth birthday party. She was drawn to his soothing voice and his intelligent conversation. He seemed genuinely interested in what she had to say and never once commented on her looks. After Beamer and A.J. established the agency she often crossed paths with the judge.

When he happened upon the spot where she often came to meditate just beyond the courthouse benches she asked him to join her. A friendship blossomed and Beamer would often call him for lunch in the park or they would take a short walk to an out of the way sushi bar. She couldn't get A.J. to stomach sushi so now she had someone to share the sushi experience with.

But sushi wasn't all that they shared. On a hot July night that past summer Beamer pulled up to her Long Island City loft and found Michael parked outside. She parked her BMW SUV and walked over to his car smiling the whole time.

She leaned into the driver's window to kiss him he seemed to want to linger onto the kiss. Beamer felt slightly dizzy and said in her southern voice "You lost sir?"

Michael smiled and kept his eyes locked on her as he got out of the car. His eyes traveled up her long legs in a short black Halston summer dress she was wearing.

He took both of her hands and looked deep into her eyes and said "Yes, you think you could help me find my way?" and kissed her again, but more passionately this time.

The kiss was intoxicating; Beamer felt light headed and leaned into him. His strong powerful hands pulled her to him and roamed over her back and shoulders. They parted for a few seconds and Beamer took his hand and led him up the stairs to her front door. She knew when she opened it there would be no turning back. Beamer somehow got the door opened and looked back at him and thought "Oh, God I want him." All she could manage to say was "Come" and he followed. Michael shed his jacket, tie and shirt along the way. She turned to him, kicked off her heels and seductively pushed the straps of her dress off of her shoulders as it easily slid to the floor in a pool around her ankles.

His erection was visible through his pants and Beamer stepped forward. She placed her hands on his to help him unbuckle his belt and push his pants down, as they kissed again. They embraced and fell on the sofa still kissing. Beamer had never felt so hot and wet at the same time. She ran her hands over his muscular arms and shoulders as he bent to suck her nipple. Beamer arched her back and a satisfying moan escaped her lips. He then ran his hand down the length of her body to her wet vagina and groaned at his discovery. Beamer rolled onto her stomach and reached into her handbag removed a condom and helped him on with it. Michael ran his tongue down her belly and lifted her legs. Beamer squirted his chin with her cum as soon as his tongue touched her clitoris and felt its warmth run between the cheeks of her ass. She cried out savagely as he proceeded to bring her to another orgasm. Now in a state of ecstasy Beamer was panting and clawing at him. He positioned himself on top of her never losing contact with her flesh, as they both read the urgency in each others eyes, he entered her slowly and she gasped and pulled closer to him as he sighed softly in her ear. There was no rush as they slowly savored the oneness of the act.

Beamer knew when she first saw him that they would either make love or fuck, there is a huge difference. When they first met and shook hands and held each others eyes her bird had chirped. She thought it was just because she was horny and had no current significant other. She secretly got off on his intellect and was captivated with his articulation. A well spoken brother is her greatest turn on. He had the Dennis Haysbert, Henry Simmons thing going on, perfect enunciation.

Michael was in his early fifties and was incredibly sexy and virile. He moved Beamer into positions ever so gracefully and coaxed several orgasms out of her. Beamer at 33 years old experienced her first multiple orgasm with a man and gave herself completely to him, a surrender that felt so right. When he finally came he called her name and the sound of it made her climax with him. He held her close, kissing her puffy lips and whispered "Thank you." A tear from her state of ecstasy rolled down her cheek, which she quickly hid, smiled and said "No, Thank you."

Micheal's anxious voice breaks Beamer out her reverie.

"Brianna?"

"Yes, darling what's up?"

"I need to see you."

"What's the matter? Everything Okay?"

"I don't want to talk over the phone, could I come by your place? Say around eight o'clock?"

"My place? I could meet you ...

"No, your place is fine."

"Okay sugar."

"See you then, bye".

A.J. walks back into the office and notices the look on Briana's face. "Is everything okay?"

"I'll see."

"All our pending cases covered?" A.J. asked as she moves towards her desk.

"Damn, I forgot, I'm supposed to tail Councilwoman's Payres boyfriend tonight."

"That snob, I'm no hater but that "sister" forgot about where she came from. I guess she's using us because she doesn't want "whitey" in her business."

"No Jay, she cornered me in court in a very ghetto tone and asked if I could stop by her office regarding a personal matter."

"When was this?" A.J. asked while clearing her desk, walking over to the mirror to primp. She finds nothing out of place and waves at herself.

Beamer watched her smiled and shook her head. A.J. is one of those women who exude confidence and is comfortable in a room full of Beamers model friends because she genuinely likes the skin she is in. She once told me "My mamma said God didn't spend any more time making you than he did me so what would make anyone better than me or me better than them?"

"I ran into her after I had to testify in the Bradshaw case."

"Just make sure she pays, A.J. says sarcastically. I've got to get to court on the Lansing matter."

"Good luck, the press is out there already and by the way. You look marvelous, darlink!!" Beamer says in an exaggerated Hollywood way.

"Why do you think I have on my power suit girl? I might come upon a photo op."

Beamer rolls her eyes at her best friend and says "Beat it ya long eared varmit."

"Okay I'm out, I'll see you at the firing range at 4:30 right?"

Beamer walks over to her and taps her. "Last tag, Love you, Smith."

A.J. tries to tag her back and misses. "Love you too, Watson." As she exits the office and catches Shenequa on a obvious personal phone call.

Shenequa quickly hangs up and picks up an incoming call, "Smith and Watson Investigations, may I help you please?" in a very professional tone. After she patches the call through, she tells A.J. that Maria and Brock, two of their other investigators are on their way back from an out of town insurance matter and would be a little late on Thursday.

"Thanks, you're doing a great job, just don't let what happened this morning happen again, O.K.?"

A.J. winks at her and Shenequa smiles back broadly while shaking her head.

All she needs is some encouragement A.J. thinks. Damn her asshole father.

Shenequa is the daughter of A.J.'s older brother Professor Klye Smith. He teaches English Literature at Queens College. A.J. and Shenequa both have a strained relationship with Kyle because Shenequa got pregnant while in her first year of college and her father insisted that she get rid of the baby.

A.J. being her only aunt and adult confidant supported her decision to keep the baby; helped her and her "baby daddy", Marcus get an apartment. She also gave Shenequa a job. and insisted that they both finish school.

Beamer buzzes Shenequa.

"Sha could you hold all calls and make sure everyone is here for the team meeting tomorrow, please. I have two reports to write, then I'm leaving to meet your Aunt okay?"

"Not a problem."

5

Later Beamer arrives home at her loft armed with a small grocery bag containing a couple of salmon steaks, new potatoes, fresh spinach and flowers for herself. She left her bike at the office and took her BMW 740 (WHAT ELSE!!) in order to shop and pick up her dry cleaning. She let herself in; deactivated the alarm walks a short distance to the kitchen; she puts the bag down and her cleaning in the hall closet and went upstairs. Beamer's loft floor is marble, light gray with black streaks. She has a spiral staircase leading up to the second story. The kitchen is just inside the foyer and decorated in stainless steel and black. Straight ahead is an impressive black wrought iron dining table with tinted sky blue glass top with six matching wrought iron chairs. A side bay window draped by slate blue tinted vertical blinds allows one to look out across the river to Manhattan; there is also a black wrought iron console table with an electric flowing rock garden bubbling on top.

Beamer was lucky enough to find a wrought iron hutch from the House Wrecking Company in Connecticut. Just beyond the dining space is a charcoal gray leather sofa and a black oak state of the art surround sound entertainment center. The guest bedroom and spare bathroom are in the rear. The spiral stairs lead up to Beamers home office, master bath, clothes room (who in the hell need an entire room for clothes) and master bedroom. Beamer heads up the stairs with her cleaning and is slightly nervous as she enters her clothes room which has shelves and racks for every item one can imagine. She carefully puts each item away. Why are you nervous girl? It's just a man? she chides herself in her three-way mirror. Beamer sits at an 18th century vanity desk she found at the Demolition Depot in Harlem and pulls off her boots. Undecided about what to put on she dons a silky pair of black lounging pants, easy to slip off, and a black dashiki with gray piping and her black fuzzy lounging heels.

Back down stairs just as she is finishing dinner and lighting dinner candles the bell chimes. Beamer runs to the foyer mirror and fluffs up her hair and opens the door. There he is in his tailored suit and looking good enough to eat. Beamer could have sworn he heard her bird chirping.

"Hi!" Beamer says with great enthusiasm.

Michael smiles brightly and says "Hello yourself" and kisses her softly on her mouth.

Yes my bird did chirp Beamer thinks.

"I hope you're hungry" Beamer says heading to the kitchen as he trails behind her. She hands him a glass of Pinot Grigio she loves to spoil herself with.

"You didn't have to cook," Michael said. He toasted his glass to hers and softly mouthed "To your health. I must admit I am starved" he said as he looked seductively in her eyes.

Beamer feels her bird squirt and knocks over her glass.

"Whoa, Michael says while helping her grab some paper towels. Their hands touch and Michael takes hers in his and says "You're shaking. Are you okay?"

Beamer looks at him and kisses him hard on the mouth. Michael breaks the kiss and says, "I've missed that."

Beamer rubbed her face against his and said "Me too." To herself she said, Oh, shit who said that.

Beamer shook the cobwebs out of her head and said "Let's eat, and hands him a small stack of chargers, napkins and silverware. Set the table, I'll bring the food and wine."

Michael smiled and reluctantly turned away.

Beamer leaned on the sink and took a deep breathe. Her bird is now wide open like a baby bird waiting to be fed a worm. Forget food she thinks. She needs to talk herself down of the ledge. Okay she says to herself, feed em, fuck em then send him on his way. Oh, didn't he come to talk. Let's put birdie in his cage and we'll talk while we eat.

She brings the wine and feels his eyes on her as she walks back to the kitchen. Up until now they haven't been alone and the sexual tension is heady. Anticipation. Beamer fixes them each healthy plates and sets them on the chargers.

"This looks delicious" he said as he placed his napkin in his lap.

"Thank you, Sir" she says in her Southern belle voice.

"You always manage to make me smile", Michael says looking at her lovingly.

They both bowed their heads and silently blessed their food.

"So, tell me what's going on?" Beamer asks as she cuts into her salmon with her fork.

"You've heard that J.R. is running for City Councilman?" J.R. is Michael Murphy, Jr. his son.

"Yes, I sent him a good luck note, he's got my vote."

"Thank you, I'm very proud of him and you know he is now going to be under the microscope."

"Yes, unfortunately your dirty laundry gets aired."

"Well, there may be a little problem with my dear daughter-in-law", he says taking a sip of his wine.

"What kind of problem?"

"Well, I'm not sure it's a problem but it was enough for Jr. to mention it to me. Chandler has a brother who is a Deputy Police Chief in Connecticut where she seems to be spending a great deal of time lately. J.R. is concerned because she is never at home, with all the celebrity parties she handles she suddenly has a need to be in Connecticut, too."

Chandler Murphy has been gaining a reputation as a major player in the world of catering and the biggest phony Beamer knows. A.J. and Beamer both agreed that, that bitch was suspect a long time ago and Jr. was too good for her.

"Really, what part of Connecticut?" she asks.

"New London."

Beamer imagines her Bugs Bunny ear stretching down to scratch her scalp again more than one bunny scratch in a day is a very bad sighn. She remains cool, it's all a state of mind people and one of the easiest things they do.

"You want me to check it out for you?"

"If it's not a problem I know you and Angelica are working on the house there. I just need to put my mind at rest."

"And protect J.R." Beamer says taking both of their plates into the kitchen. When she reappears at the kitchen doorway she is butt ass naked except for her fuzzy heels.

"Ready for dessert?" she asks while sucking on her finger looking shy.

Michael wipes his mouth with his napkin and knocks the chair over as he stands loosening his tie. Beamer walks over to the stairwell goes halfway up and kneels on a step and looks over her shoulder while lifting her left ass cheek giving him an invitation he couldn't refuse. He walks toward her thinking, such sweet candy, climbs the stairs behind her and licks her from clit to ass, which makes her shutter. She looks back, moans pulling him up by his chin and licks her juices from his mouth. Beamer backs up the stairs and leads him to her double wide gray and black marble shower stall where she helped him undress along the way. She turns on the steam and adjusts the water while he is behind her kissing her neck. She steps into the shower and lets the water run through her wild mane. Michael stepped in front of her, closed the door and kissed her full in the mouth. Beamer lets out a moan and arches her back. Michael released her lips to caress kiss and catches her nipple in his mouth. His strong build and muscular brawn and height excite her; not to mention that this man knows exactly how to touch her, he needs neither training nor instruction. Michael switches to lick her other nipple while holding her back with one arm and her ass in the other, Beamer humps his thigh. Michael lets out a small chuckle sensing her wanting and says "Yes baby here you go" he turns her around, her breast to the shower door and exposed to the view of the mirrored wall. He savors watching her enjoy her orgasm and tries to drain her of them. Their pace picks up and she says "Yes, baby fuck me good" and starts to climax. Michael pulls out and comes on her ass and holds her up as he senses her legs giving away. He eases her down on his knee and lets the water run over them both as he caresses her with soothing strokes. Michael reaches for soap and a loofah sponge and starts washing her lightly. He stands her up to rinse her, opens the shower door, grabs a towel drapes it around her and carries her to her bedroom. Beamer stretches and purrs like a cat. Or was that her kitty-cat purring. Michael kisses her full on the lips and says, "Don't move". He returns to the shower and rinses himself off.

Michael joins her in the bed and kisses her and tells her not to move again. Impulsively Beamer sits up to watch him walk away and whistles and shakes her head. Michael returns with her Body Butter from the Body Shop. He towels her dry and massages her entire body in the elixir. She lotions him down in return then she slips on her fuzzy heels and goes down stairs to get their unfinished wine. Their eyes lock and they both put their glasses on the nightstands as Beamer reaches in the drawer for a condom and kiss deeply. They both wanted more. Beamer rolls over on him and caresses him as she sucks his nipples. She rubs her labia along the length of his throbbing dick as he reaches to insert himself into her. She stops him and pins his arms down playfully. She concentrates her focus again on his nipples and continues to ride him giving herself a small orgasm. He moans. Beamer then lifts one knee up and slides up and down on his dick. They release satisfying groans as she settles down and shutters. Michael lifts his head and takes a nipple in his mouth and reaches around to massage her ass. Beamer moans and pulls her nipple free; it's as hard as a pebble.

She kisses him and humps down faster and harder as his finger, wet from her juices slips into her ass. They look into each others eyes and he tells her to hold on. Beamer puts her arms around his neck as he proceeds to hump her with a new intensity. Beamer is close to the edge and bites his shoulder Michael lets out a guttural sound as Beamer claws him slightly. Both are drenched in sweat. They kiss as they both cum and collapse in an exhausted heap. His throbbing dick is still inside of her and when it slips out she moans, "No!" Michael laughs that sexy laugh of his and says "Don't worry, there's more."

Beamer is lying on his chest as he is stroking her back and kissing her face and shoulders. Beamer looks into his eyes and says "What is this madness, Sir?" She says in her southern belle voice.

"It's pure pleasure."

"I knew this would happen."

"I always thought about it, it was better than I imagined."

"I wanted it so bad."

"Good and I wanted you. You sure know how to make an old man feel young again. You are such an enthusiastic lover and could easily break my heart. I value our friendship and want nothing more than to see you when I can. I know a beautiful young woman like your self …

Beamer puts a finger to his lips to hush

him and says "I have a predilection for older men and your naiveté regarding your allure absolutely turns me on."

"Wow", Michael says blushing kissing her lips. "I was honored to have you as my friend and now as a lover; this he says, pulling her closer, is gravy."

Beamer makes a face "Gravy" she says acting insulted and clutching her imaginary pearls, I'd rather be a chocolate sundae."

Michael replies "Mmmmm, dessert" and rolls over on top of her.

6

The next day Beamer comes bouncing into the office the wearing a black form fitting light weight knit sweater dress by Michelle and black David Aaron boots carrying a six pack of gourmet donuts. She stopped and purchased a dozen for the building security guards and a six pack for Shenequa who is listening to Ella Fitzgerald.

"Here's your fix girl" she says to A.J. placing the box on her desk.

The donuts are a payment for A.J.'s superior marksmanship at the range. A.J. had worn a chocolate, suede patchwork short skirt suit, by Monique a private designer at Brooklyn, NY and chocolate Kenneth Cole pumps. A.J. takes some napkins and spreads several in her lap and says "Sore loser."

"I'll get you next time" Beamer says plopping down at her desk.

A.J. sticks her tongue out at Beamer as Beamer steals a donut and shoves it whole into her mouth.

"You are absolutely glowing this morning" A.J. says.

Teena Marie's "I Need Your Lovin" is playing in the background.

"It's a new overnight renew cream I'm using and several of the intense orgasms I experienced with Mr. Murphy last evening" Beamer says with her hand on her bosom in a southern belle drawl. Then back to ghetto, "girl do I have an earful for you."

"Give me all the nasty details" A.J. says wiping her mouth and rubbing her hands together.

"Are we taking on the Phenom assignment?"

"I wanted to discuss that with you I called him last night and told him we would. I started feeling sorry for the young brother. You okay with it?"

"Sure Softie!"

"Well, your phone was going straight to voice mail, so I figured you were busy. He also invited us to his team meeting for a "Blue Skyies" celebration he is holding at the Retro; oh, and he's pretty sure the disc was recorded in his suite there. I suggested we operate under the guise of security for the affair."

"That's what's up. This means a new outfit, hmmm, what to wear. Okay focus, focus Beamer, to herself, "I made dinner for Michael and he wants me to check up on something for him."

"Looks like he helped himself to you, I

swear you look like you're eighteen again!"

"Will you stop! "This is serious."

"Okay. Would this something interfere with our taking on the Phenom assignment?"

"No, but we could kill two birds with one stone. It seems Chandler is spending a great deal of time in Connecticut and supposedly with her brother. Her brother who is Deputy Police Chief in New London, of all places, and they never got along, so Michael is suspicious."

"Get out! I guess our favorite little sleepy town is not so sleepy after all. I smell the stink already."

"Every little town has something nefarious going on from the Alderman wearing the Mexican nanny's panties to the Mayor having married the ex-stripper, honey-child."

"So what do you say we go snooping in New London?"

"Sounds like a plan Sherlock" Beamer says stuffing another donut in her mouth.

"My, aren't we talented! Did a lot of that last night?"

"I've been told by a select few gentlemen that I am the best." Doing her Bugs Bunny champion fist clenched wave over her head.

A.J. rolls her eyes and says under her

breath, that's what you think. Mr. Johnson may have something to say about that when I get to Connecticut, she thinks to herself. I could use a fix myself.

Beamer buzzes Shenequa, "Could you track down Joe-Joe for me?" she asks.

"No problem."

"Thank you, maam."

"You're welcome" Shenequa says.

"Good thinking. He can do his usual scoping out of the situation and the potential cast of characters."

Joseph Woo is Beamers ex-body guard and their guardian angel. He's like the Shadow and shit; he always shows up when their asses are in a jam. Joseph is a former government operations specialist who was injured in a covert assignment. His uncle is Tiki, the famous designer used Beamer exclusively when she modeled. He and Beamer both come from mixed lineage; his parents, Anna Walker and Joseph Woo are renowned restaurateurs.

Joe speaks perfect English and is fluent in Spanish, French and Chinese. He is a man of very few words and makes A.J. nervous as hell. She admitted that he makes her bird chirp and he calls her Bo-boy (pronounced Beau-Boy and means my precious or my darling). But A.J.

doesn't know that. Beamer gets a kick out of how much it flusters A.J., because she thinks she is so cool. Joe is shrouded in mystery and is GQ fine. Joseph is also Mr. Spy Shop himself; always up on the latest gadgets; affectionately they call him Felix with his bag of tricks. He recently gave Beamer a butterfly brooch with a microscopic camera installed and she is anxious to use it.

The rest of the Smith and Watson Investigation Team are expected to report to Beamer upon arrival. Charo Menendez is a drop-dead gorgeous brick house retired detective and good friend of Angelica's. Rashaad Williamson was a paralegal, one-armed wannabee sleuth who lost his arm protecting Uncle Smitty. He is also their computer whiz, specializing in background checks, criminal histories and anything else you don't want known. Brock Pellegrino a lawyer who was disbarred by the ABA for lying to protect his no-good son. He's a bruiser who keeps them just above the law and word is he knows how to touch a girl.

Shenequa buzzed and announced that Joe is on the line.

"What's up brother?" Beamer asks reclining in her chair.

"Same old thing, sister. What you got?" Joe asks.

"Feel like riding up to Connecticut?" she asks.

"You finish the renovations?"

"No, it's a case, but it's in the same area."

"Uh-oh there goes the neighborhood."

"Well its two separate issues so I need to fill you in before you leave. You got plans for dinner?"

"Yes, I'm eating some fine young thing this evening" he says playfully.

"Just make sure the job is thorough, you know what I told you about how us ladies feel about you guys playing with your food."

"Breakfast"?

"Sure, at our spot?" Beamer asks.

"I'll be there; 8:30 good?"

"You bet! See you, love you."

"Love you more" Joe said hung up.

7

The city of New London, CT has become renowned for the newly renovated $19 million dollar Waterfront Park. But most importantly, it is infamous for being the landing spot for the Amistad slave ship.

A.J. and Beamer had a chance to explore the ship while it was docked in Mystic, CT, a favorite haunt of ours. The ladies usually go up to the Norwich Spa; they believe in the art of pampering themselves, they visit the Mystic Marine Life Aquarium; do some fine dining and visit the wine vineyards. It's their own special therapy.

The Amistad tells the story of Sengbe Pieh, aka "Cinque" a slave who was kidnapped from Sierra Leone in 1839 "Cinque" used a loose nail to pick the lock on his shackles, thereby, freeing himself and 52 others who had also been kidnapped. With a machete he killed his captors. The mutinied ship sailed for days in the wrong direction before finally being spotted by a U.S. Navy boat off the coast of Long Island and towed to New London's pier. The trials that ensued were a preamble to the conflict that would lead to Civil War in 1861. Since Steven Spielberg's 1997 adaptation exposed the story to the masses the Amistad has been "touring" the Eastern Seaboard since the summer of 2001.

The experience was extremely moving for Beamer and A.J. They teared up and, Beamer could not stay below ship, she the small space was suffocating. They hope that educational institutions, parents and others ensure that the children of the world and in particular African American children know the history of the Amistad.

Beamer and A.J. arrived in Connecticut a day later; it was a crisp sunny Friday morning; they checked into a two-bedroom suite at the Radisson in New London. A.J. was feeling some "type of way", anticipation, the entire ride. The ladies usually play some old school hits on the way up but A.J. was in the mood for some jazzy love tunes like Richard Elliot's "Sweet Surrender". She was smiling silently to herself the entire ride. Besides the driver gets music preference and Beamer is no hater. She knows what's up with her partner. They both are in casual wear. Beamer is rocking a black velour sweat suit by Sean Jean with her hair in two big pony tails and A.J. has on a burgundy two piece lounging outfit by Douglas Says.

The ride Northeast this time of the year is spectacular; the foliage (the color representation of the fall leaves, for those buffoons who have no clue) is breathtaking.

They were meeting Joseph for dinner. They had reservations at the Radisson in New London because of the indoor heated pool. Beamer was going to sneak a power nap because she knew A.J. would be M.I.A (missing in action) for a minute. All girls should take a nappy-nap when they can. As soon as they entered the room Beamer sprayed the bathroom down with Lysol, after the 60 Minute special on hotel germs both ladies were always sure to spray the sheets, sink, toilet, shower, phone and remote. A.J. has the drapes drawn and is looking out intently she then pulls out her cell phone and calls a programmed number.

A male voice answers, "Hello."

"I'm here."

I'm tending to the fish, see you in a minute."

Stephen Johnson was a New York City cop who left the job because he hit the lottery for $12 million dollars!!!!. He always wanted to hook up with A.J. but, she did not want to mix business with pleasure and because she valued their friendship too much. Also she couldn't chance becoming the precinct whore just because she wanted to fuck a few guys. Men can have every woman in the precinct, but you let a chick try that shit and you become used goods. After Stephen hit the lottery he worked two more years to get his full twenty-year retirement pension. He then retired and gave A.J. one-half million dollars. He always said he would if he hit and he asked her out on a date. A.J. told him the date she had in mind would last all weekend and she would make all the plans. It had nothing to do with money, she just wanted to do him plain and simple.

They took a trip to Mystic, CT where she introduced him to the world of Bed and Breakfasts and sharing baths in big old cat paw bathtubs. Stephen who had always been a class act, loved Eastern Connecticut and built a home in Stonington, CT in hopes of enticing her to move there with him. He owns a beautiful five-bedroom home, a Jag, a Navigator and is most proud of the small private aquarium he built. Stephen is basically chilling waiting for A.J. to come to her senses and move in with him.

He's everything she wants but can't handle, not now anyway. He's sensitive, kind-hearted, handsome, sexy, spontaneous, dedicated, attentive and faithful. He smothers A.J. so she stays in the city to keep in control of her life and he understands and tolerates it.

A.J. removes a summer dress from her overnight bag and goes into the bathroom.

Beamer strips right there and took her bathing suit out of her overnight bag and steps into it. Being a model has made her immodest to changing in front of other people. A.J. on the other hand is a little stiff about it.

8

The ride to Stephens seems to take forever but it helps A.J. to collect her cool ass as she takes the scenic route. Connecticut is a scenic wonderland. She has changed into a modest but shapely olive t-shirt dress with three-quarter sleeves, it's a Bloomingdales original and olive Charles David 3 inch mules. She pulls up into the driveway, cuts off the ignition and looks in all of her mirrors. She notices Stephen has a new neighbor. The land across from his home was being developed the last time she was there. A police cruiser is parked in the driveway. As A.J. starts to primp in the visor mirror a man emerges from the house followed by two women. Wouldn't it be her luck that one of the women is Chandler Murphy.

The man walks them to one of the cars parked in his driveway and he waits for them to pull out before he goes inside the house. Now what's going on here she wondered. The man must be her brother as he favors her in looks. A.J. rechecks her mirror she spots Joe Woo off in the distant wooded area surrounding the house. Probably following Chandler.

What most people don't know about private eyeing is that most cases are solved through persistence, instinct and dumb luck. Mostly luck. Knowing he will have information for them later A.J. shimmies off her panties, checks her face in the mirror and winks.

As she inhales the smell of exotic flowers and chlorine from the pool she notices how clean everything is. One of reasons A.J. can only take this man in small doses is his obsession with cleanliness. She's no slob but this could be a "Sleeping with the Enemy" case. A.J. loves this house and Stephen, it was built with her in mind. All of the things she wanted in a home were there, waiting. The master bedroom is on the back of the house and enclosed entirely in glass. Remote controlled blinds can shade the room for privacy if you want some. You can jump right out of bed and into an Olympic size pool.

The sound of the door opening causes him look up. She heard his voice as she was approaching; apparently he was talking to his babies (the exotic fish), it's a ritual. Their eyes lock and her stomach immediately starts to ache, her bird is drooling with anticipation. He smiled that sly sideways smile and puts away the special foods he needs for the fish. Taking off his gloves he goes to wash his hands. Everything's so damn, clean. A.J. admires a few fish along the way and tried to remain cool when she knew better. You could feel the electricity in the air. He turns to face her and pulls his wife beater off. He has on sweats. Good she thinks.

"Baby, how are you?" he says opening his arms to receive her.

"Better now" she says holding him tight.

A.J. puts her panties, which she had wadded up in her hand into his hand. He looked at them smiled. He brought them to his face to smell them and said, Aah.

She reaches up and pulls him by his neck to kiss him. The kiss is hard and hungry. There will be time for the nice and slow loving later.

Stephen breaks the kiss and sucks her neck. She cradles his head as he pulls up her dress and squeezes her ass. He loves her perfect round behind. His mouth moves back to hers and his hands explore and finds her soaked. He lifts her dress up over her head, picks her up and carries her over to the sterile stainless steel worktable, opens the bottom cabinet pulls out a towel. All with one hand, Hercules! Hercules! He put her down and positions her legs with her knees bended on the edge of the table. He has a full view of her and said "pretty pussy" and stoops to lap at her like an ice cream cone. A.J. is in ecstasy, but she can't wait and cums. She pulls his head up and says "gimme now".

She slides off the table and gets a condom out of her bag, rips the wrapper with her teeth, hands it to him. She bent over the table looks back at him and says "Come fuck this pussy, this is what you been waiting for right?" He pulls his hard dick out and A.J. licks her lips.

"Oh, you make me crazy when you talk like that".

He enters her slowly all the while looking in her eyes with vulnerability that she loves and catches his breath.

"Yes, baby nice and slow, open that pussy up with that big dick" A.J. says.

"Yes, baby. You miss this dick?"

Not so fast mister I'm running this show. A.J. thought to herself, so she never answers when he asks her that.

He sinks his mouth into her neck and she pushes back as his hand reaches around and rubs her clitoris. She used to be embarrassed because she was so sensitive there and gets so wet, but Stephen taught her to go with her natural body reaction. She learned to make her orgasms something very personal and enjoys having them.

"Ah yes, A.J., I miss this sweet pussy so much" he said ramming into her.

"Yes, show me baby."

They both come quickly and loudly. She

shuddered. She's not disappointed because for round two he turns into the Energizer Bunny Rabbit. He picks her up and carries her through the greenhouse outside and into his bed. She is spent. He wipes the sweat off of her brow, kisses her forehead and cradles her in his arms.

"Take five baby, that's all you gonna get" because it's been to long and you got work to do" he said caressing her ass.

"Mmmmm" she hummed and smiled; it was all she could manage.

9

That night A.J. and Beamer drove into Mystic and dined at Go Fish. Fine dining is a luxury both ladies take pleasure in and consider a blessing. Go Fish in the Ye Olde Shopping Village also has a wine selection to die for. Forget Hennessey, Alize and Cristal. A fine wine is what's up, Beamer used to date a Wine Master who educated the ladies about buying, collecting and selecting wines for meals. There is a wine for everything from appetizers and soup to dessert.

A.J. has on a crisp white blouse with turned up cuffs and black flare leg dress slacks; she is wearing her grandma's pearl earrings. Beamer has on a black cotton and polyester jumpsuit that attracts stares as they linger near the headwaiters post. Two white businessmen at the bar in their early 40's check them out and nod hello. They smile back. When did they get so bold? Beamer is used to it and A.J. finds it interesting and never knows what to say when approached by one. Everybody wants a taste of chocolate. The head waiter, Bradley greets them warmly pecking each of their cheeks.

"Ah, the two most exciting women I know" he says with his hand on his heart.

"Bradley, how are you?" the ladies say in

unison.

"Bradley, darling we need a table for three, is that okay?" Beamer says placing her hand on his forearm.

"Now that I have seen my reason for being, I can as you ladies say, exhale," Bradley says picking up three menus and takes them to the best seats in the house.

"Is this table to your liking or do you ladies require some privacy?" he said all hush-hush like. Bradley is aware of what they do and has utilized their services himself to catch his cheating wife and keep his restaurant. It's also very useful to have an ear wherever you hang out.

"This is perfect; maybe we can share a Sambuka after dinner?" A.J. said. Bradley bows and says "Your wish is my command."

A.J. sees Joseph come in and all the women in the restaurant watch him. Imagine what a Chinese and a Jamaican mixed looks like? Whoa!, Mouth watering, tasty, finger licking, a juicy morsel.

For appetizers they ordered fried wonton stuffed with crab meat and sautéed spinach. For an entrée A.J. had the chicken breast stuffed with crabmeat, lobster and scallops twice whipped potatoes and more spinach. The ladies also are big Popeye the Sailor fans. Joe ordered baked salmon with couscous and string beans with carrots. Beamer ordered the Mahi-mahi with sautéed vegetables and yellow rice.

They shared two bottles of an utterly fabulous Pino Grigio Candonini with dinner.

"A.J. you look great how's hubby?" Beamer said.

"Oh, now you're gonna try and fuck with me, right."

"Your skin is glowing" Joe says.

A.J. drops her fork and repositions it in the attack position. Beamer and Joe share a laugh.

A.J. turned to Joe and said "And here I thought you liked me" trying to look hurt.

"I adore you and wish for a chance to show you" Joe said very seriously.

A.J. coughs while sipping her wine. Joseph jumps up to pat her on the back.

"Something is afoot here in little old New London" Joe said.

"I know you saw Chandler yesterday, you see anything else?" A.J. says wondering if he observed her and Stephen. Feeling some type of way, about possibly being watched, nasty girl.

Joe looks at A.J. and holds her eyes, knowing what she means by the little sly grin on her face.

"Saw Chandler." Where?" Beamer said sipping her Pinot.

"At the new house across from Stephen, who ever built it must have hit the lotto also." They're going to have to rename the street millionaire's row". A.J. says.

"It's owned by her brother, Charles who is a law enforcement officer here."

"I know their mother left them well off but, I didn't think that well; then sighing "Oh, Lord not another dirty cop" Beamer said.

Joe lifts his wine glass in salute. "I guess we'll find out won't we."

Bradley reappears to remove their plates himself and offer dessert.

Joe plays with his blackberry-cabernet sorbet on the spoon with his tongue and A.J. shifts uncomfortably in her seat.

"Is that what you did last night?" Beamer says asks sitting back and folding her arms waiting for a response.

"A gentleman never kisses and tells" Joe says very seriously. "Besides ancient Chinese secret and all that shit."

They all share a laugh.

For dessert the three of them shared a chocolate pagoda. Three heavenly blocks of exotic chocolate, layered with thin slices of chocolate cake and melted chocolate adorned like a Chinese temple. Brilliant! With this they had a snort of sweet orange liquor.

Beamer stuck her tongue out at Joe and

caught Bradley's eye "Check please, and we'll meet you at the bar."

After they grilled Bradley about the new local millionaires they proceed to the parking lot.

A man pulls up on a Harley Davidson and nearly clipped Joe. Joe turned to face him in a defensive stance as the stranger dismounted his ride. The man moved with such stealth that the next thing they knew the two were both in karate stances ready to face off.

"Hold up, what the hell is going on?" Beamer said while she took a karate stance, ready to help. A.J. had her gun drawn and by her side.

The two men grabbed each other hugged, patted each other on the back and laugh.

"You know you were going down? Don't you?" the stranger says with a slight accent.

"Bullshit, how are you man?"

"Ahem" Beamer feigns clearing her throat.

The stranger had turned to face them. He is at least 6' tall and had steely thighs, with an exotic caramel complexion, jet-black wavy hair that he ran his fingers through in a effort to fix it. His eyes were cat grey.

A.J. says through her teeth so only Beamer can hear "Gulp".

"Mikel Hassan, I would like you to meet my sisters, Angelica and Brianna, or A.J. and

Beamer."

"Ladies" he makes a slight bow, then takes A.J.'s hand and kisses the back of it and places a slightly longer kiss on Beamers.

When their eyes meet Beamers bird starts blowing bubbles and her nipples grew hard. She had never been this aroused by just looking into a man's eyes. She and A.J. talked about it happening but this was way over the top. CHIRP!!!!!!!

"Joe, you never told me you had such beautiful sisters."

"The fact that you two poster boys know each other is criminal" A.J. said.

"Well, we all sort of grew up together." This was usually his standard answer for not having to explain how this motley crew got together. "Ladies, Special Liaison to the Police Department Inspector Hassan will be our go to guy if things get sticky."

"Joseph has briefed me and I have been assigned by the local prosecutor's office. I hope you don't mind my tagging along to ensure no laws are broken. And I can assist in the apprehension and arrest of your extortionist; but most importantly, ensure you ladies are safe" Mickel said, his eyes still locked with Beamers.

"Thanks, I was going to try to schmooze the local police but you know how they can give

P.I.'s a hard time, former brethren or not" says A.J.

"Joe could bring you to the meeting were having tomorrow" Beamer said. She wondered what his heritage is maybe Russian and African or maybe Ghanese and English.

"Tomorrow, when?" his eyes still locked on Beamer.

"10:00 am at the Retro" Beamer said.

"Perhaps if you don't have any breakfast plans I could take you for a ride. There are some beautiful sights here, but I'm sure none compare to your beauty."

Beamer laughs a laugh neither A.J. nor Joe has ever heard before. They both look at each other warily, Joe then crossed his eyes.

"That would be most exciting Sir, as I consider myself quite the rider. We could talk shop as you me say" Beamer replies in her southern belle voice, with her hand at her throat as if clutching her pearls.

"Then perhaps you could ride me?"

Beamer and A.J. look at each other and said simultaneously under their breath "Too easy."

"Why, Sir", Beamer responds, "we've only just made our acquaintances, yet I cannot turn down such a titillating offer. We're staying at the Radisson in New London. I'll be outside at 8:00, is that good?"

"Perfect" he says, bows to A.J. and kisses Beamers hand again gets on his bike and rides off.

"Who was that masked man? Girl, fuck the shit out of him first chance you get" A.J. says out loud. "Oops", covering her mouth embarrassed that Joe heard her say such an unlady-like thing aloud. "So, tomorrow we meet Phenom at the Retro" she adds in an effort to steer the conversation back to business.

"I knew you had it in you" Joe say walking away.

"Let's roll loser." Beamer says as they get into the car. She hits the CD play button and Rick James "Give It To Me Baby" comes on.

"Takes one to know one" A.J. says dancing in her seat.

10

The Retro Casino located in Gales Ferry, CT opened six months ago. It celebrates old world style; Vegas gaudy lighting and all. The uniforms worn by the staff are right out of the sixties; and their main attraction is a version of the Folies Bergere, the quintessential Vegas showgirl extravaganza. The hotel/casinos suites are styled in the décor of a Rubik's cube, black, white, red, yellow, green and blue plastic, acrylic and vinyl everywhere.

When they walk into the lobby Phenom is giving Joe and Mikel his spiel about modeling as Joe looks up and waves them over. Phenom is wearing a black velour sweat suit and his new sneakers.

"I see you've met my brother and our number one man" Beamer said.

"Yo, I had no idea, dude was down with y'all. I was trying to get him to be in the campaign for my new line of men suits. Not that you can't now" he says giving Joe his card.

Joe takes it and smirks. Little did Phenom know that Joe has been approached from the time he was twelve to model, he never has and never will. A well dress black man walks by heading towards the conference room.

As they head toward the conference room, "TV One" is interviewing Keyshawn Strong outside the nearby entrance to the Retro Arena where the celebrity charity ball game was held the previous night. Keyshawn, a former pro baller and teammate of Ducal Davis now manages Phenom's street ball team. He was banned from the league for violating part of the collective bargaining agreement "3 strike rule". Since Keyshawn was close to Davis Ducal, Phenom paid for his last rehab stint. So far he has kept his shenanigans out of the news. With him was the rapper John Dough, singer Sammy David, Jr. Both are all on the Project Record label a handsome European looking man in a sharp suit is with them.

"What's up slick?" the suit yells to Phenom.

The conference room is decorated with a large teardrop shaped acrylic orange table with white, yellow, and red chairs. The lighting is yellow, white and orange. A light buffet is set up for those who wish to partake.

Next to Phenom is his personal assistant Mya a 40 year old beauty who was rumored to be his one time lover and mentor; Mimi, Phenom's sister, who handles Phenomenal Records Marketing and Promotions; Booker T. Jones his main confidant, business partner and Larissa's brother. Booker spends a great deal of time partying and looking for a photo op. Also present is Spenser Hornsby, the suit, Phenom's attorney and publicist and Chandler Murphy. She is there because she is handling the catering, not once does she make eye contact with A.J. or Beamer. Bodyguards Lex and Kyle take up post behind Phenom at the left and right corners of the room.

Phenom is impressive as a leader and has all his bases covered. He stresses that this years gala is for the prosperous year that they had and the theme "Blue Skies" represents all good things in the future. The newly developed Phenomenal Things division has partnered with "Bloo Vodka" and the new PhenomX sneaker. Phenom then mentions the additional security people not mentioning Beamer, A.J. or Joe by name just pointing them out as he explains that the security team will all be wearing silver wristbands.

"Why we need extra security?" Bookers booming voice protest.

"Because. I want it!" Phenom says unwaveringly.

"And the man gets what he wants" Spenser said in a tone that could have been taken as being toadyish or sarcastic.

Phenom ignores the comment and continues to go around the table. Booker is giving him the daggers stare until he realizes that A.J. is watching then he smiles, winks and blows a kiss at her. She rolls her eyes.

Meanwhile, Lex at 6’5” and 300lbs. is trying to give Beamer his meanest stare but softens his gaze and gave her a quick wink when her matching stare doesn’t falter. Beamer’s bird stirs slightly as she caught Mikel watching this exchange. He had been all business up til that moment and had not acknowledged her.

After the meeting, Phenom, Joe, A.J., Mikel and Beamer head up to the penthouse suite to watch the disc. Booker catches up to them and says “Yo, wait for me, kid.”

“Yo, I’ll catch up to you later” Phenom says and gives him a pound.

As they headed toward the elevator A.J. looks back to see Booker giving Phenom that hateful stare again.

Mikel whispers something to Joe and then got off the elevator on the next floor, but not before squeezing Beamers hand.

11

The penthouse suite is adorned with black and white marble tile, a red sofa, a yellow chaise lounge and two blue acrylic double chairs. They enter the bedroom and Phenom goes behind a photo of Marilyn Monroe; opens a wall safe and takes out a disc and hands it along with the remote to A.J.

"You have that list of names of your people who need room keys, Phenom asked A.J. acting fidgety. I can get them while you do your thing."

They realized he doesn't want to be there when they start watching the tape. A.J., Joe and Beamer on the bed which has a multi-colored checkered spread. After Phenom left, Joe took the disc from A.J. inserts it and sits back down next to Beamer, who has the remote. She turns the television on and pressed play.

Davis Ducal, the "Double Dee" is on his knees behind Larissa fucking her with long slow strokes, his penis is thick and at least 8 inches.

"Yeah, baby, do that shit," he said slapping Larissa on the ass. She moaned.

Larissa was eating Mimi's pussy like a man would and should, she had her lips parted and is licking every crevice. Mimi is pulling her hair, wailing and bucking her hips wildly.

Davis starts pumping harder and Larissa also picks up her pace. Mimi then sat up and announced "I need some dick". Davis pulls out of Larissa, as she and Mimi kiss, lies on his back and Mimi mounts him and Larissa sits on his face.

"That's the girl I saw with Chandler yesterday" A.J. says.

"Looks like the recorder was there", Beamer says pointing to an étagère against the wall.

Joe noticed that they all crossed and uncrossed their legs several times and chuckled.

"What's so funny?" A.J. asks.

"Nothing, you had to be there" Joe says thinking of his date the night before.

They watched the entire tape and rewound it several times to the blowjob scene. Because, Mimi swallows Davis's dick whole. Joe also rewound the tape several times.

They heard the penthouse door to open and close; and stop the disc to talk to Phenom.

"Here are the room keys you need and the gala passes for your crew, he said while fidgeting again. You find out anything that might be helpful."

"We don't have a crew we have a team" A.J. says curtly then adds, "Larissa is suspect"

"She continually looked up in the cameras

direction and once, I was certain she smiled at it" Joe said.

"You think my sister knew?" he asks obviously seething.

"Probably not, but we'll see who knows what when we talk to them tomorrow" Beamer says.

"So, that ho is trying to play me?"

"Do not confront them until after we have talked to them. If one of them is behind this you can't let on that you suspect something. We only told you now so you can get over your initial anger."

"Relax, Davis has been gone a minute so let's see what the motivation is behind doing this" Joe says.

"Relax!, that's easier said than done, man. Motive, money and embarrassing my sister." he says pacing back and forth.

"Let me talk to him a sec", A.J. said to Joe and Beamer, I'll meet you in the lobby so we can go back and get ourselves and everyone settled."

Joe's cell phone rings he answers it and listens. "That was Mikel, he thinks we should have Rashaad run Bookers cell phone, just to be safe."

"Aw, this shit keeps getting worse" Phenom exclaims.

"Let's step in the other room" A.J says to

Phenom.

“No problem, Beamer said, I’ll get our stuff. You hang out here. See if you can get us an appointment for a massage before tonight.”

“You should probably get one too, man” Joe said to Phenom as he gave him a pound before they depart.

Phenom walks over to the picture size window in the bedroom and looks out.

A.J. walked up behind him and couldn’t help for feeling sorry for him and puts her hand on his forearm briefly.

“Look you said you want to represent and maintain the image of a positive black man who made it out of the ghetto; you need to keep a cool head. Whoever is doing this, your sister and/or her friend, is obviously in my experience in a precarious situation. You being the smart business man I think you are, he turns to face her, you could save me some time and yourself some money by giving me any information on any or all of your employees whom you think maybe capable of trying to pull this off. Tomorrow, when we talk to our featured stars, he smiles, you can go off all you want but, we will need to track their movements immediately after. You also need to think about the authorities getting involved at some point because; this thing will come to a head. I know some people who maybe of assistance and discreet. I'm going to have two of my people, in addition to Joe, not wear the silver wristband pass and watch Mimi and Larissa, let's see if there are any clandestine goings-on and if you can obtain their cell phone numbers that would be helpful."

"I ain't tryin to have no drama that's going to give me bad press. I'm a grown man now, he said with clinched fist, I've worked to damn hard."

"Well, you know my mama always said "the devil is busy" so recognize this for what it is and hope for a peaceful resolution."

"You know I always thought you were so smart. That I, he pauses looking at the floor, that I could never be anything until that day you gave your speech about being a proud black person." He takes a step in her personal space but not making any eye contact, "I had the hugest crush on you. And I realized that's the reason I acted out so badly. I thought you were so beautiful; he paused took a deep breath as if getting up his nerve; looking deep into her eyes, and you still are."

Gulp! That's all A.J. can think of is "Good Grief!" and "Yikes!" Whenever younger men approach her she says to herself "Run along little one, before I am lying somewhere rubbing my stomach, picking my teeth with your bones."

Chirp!

A.J. changed her stance hoping her body language would put him off, folding her arms in front of her chest and wanting to defeather her bird for acting out.

Before she could respond there's a knock at the door.

Phenom is still staring at her as if waiting for her to respond.

"You should get that, and then, under her breath, Thank you Jesus."

Phenom walks over to the door and she can't help but watch him.

Chirp!

That's it, someone is getting showers all week, no baths, she chides herself.

No sooner than he opened the door Beamer rushed in, "I need the car keys silly", giving A.J. a wink.

A.J. fishes them out her bag and holds on to them "I'm ready, she then faced Phenom and asks, "You cool."

"Yeah, I'm good", he says, giving her a sly smile.

They turned to leave when Beamer turns back to him and says "I know you know your people so think about whom Larissa spends time with and their situation. Maybe she has an accomplice."

"That will be a mighty long list" Phenom says.

After they got on the elevator Beamer said to her "Okay, this is getting scary, were you sending out rescue signals?"

"Yes!, and you came right on time, just like a good bitch should."

"Something told me don't leave, I just felt uneasy for you. Joe said I was crazy."

"Let's just hope that your radar is working when my black ass is in a real jam."

"Is it me or was their some sexual tension in the air?"

"Just some school boy crush he admitted to."

"Well that school boy has an awfully loaded looking package. That man should be arrested for wearing sweats," Beamer says.

"He is sexy and could make your bird feel some type of way, I especially liked the way he handled himself at the meeting earlier."

"Yeah, he could get some, in another life and the fact that we are talking about it makes my head hurt" A.J. says.

"Great, the Spa has openings in an hour for massages. We could run back to the Radisson, get our stuff, get a massage and take a power nap before we drop it like it's hot."

12

A.J. has on deep navy Focus 2000 pants with a cuff. They are a perfect fit. She is wearing a baby blue 3/4 sleeve wrap shirt, and a navy blue onyx stone encrusted bracelet from Ilsa Majeres in Mexico. Beamer has on a midnight blue, practically black wrap jumpsuit. And she looks good enough to eat. Joe is wearing a perfect powder blue shirt and navy Armani pants, Phenom is in his ear again. The D.J. is played old school music and everyone danced. Phenom announces that "if no one wants to dance then they should leave the tent, they'll be no standing around, this a celebration."

The first tent was set up with cafeteria-style tables with blue china and sterling silverware. The high back chairs are covered in midnight blue velvet with silver tulle bows tied around the back. As soon as you are seated a waiter appears to read you the selections and bring your choice of drink. Tattinger's champagne bottles are on ice at every table in silver ice buckets. On the menu was of course New England Clam Chowder, sautéed string beans, garlic corn with red and orange peppers, Scallops with lobster custard, Jumbo Shrimp with snow peas and exotic mushrooms, Lobster Cassoulet, Curried Chicken and Chateaubriand.

Chandler Murphy is darting in and out of the kitchen giving orders and chatting with the guest.

On the dance floor Charo and her husband were making a scene to Van McCoy's "Do The Hustle". Brock and his fiance Salina, another supermodel, are slow dancing. What? Love makes people crazy' they probably hear their own music. "Love Thang" come on and Beamer and A.J. both throw there hands in the air and start to dance. Project Records artist Sammy David, Jr., John Dough and Keyshawn are watching them riveted. Phenom comes over and takes A.J.'s hand leading her to the dance floor. Only because she doesn't want to embarrass him in front of his boys she didn't walk away. A.J. looks over a Beamer who is grinning from ear to ear and still dancing by herself. This was their favorite old school song and they didn't hold back. Combining a bit of old school and new dance moves they made quite an impression, they ain't hardly trying to "drop it like it's hot"; "lean back" or do some damn country ass "snap back" move.

Joe comes up behind Beamer and does a very cool two step and she backs up on him. Her small fan club now requires a maintenance crew to clean up all their drool. Beamer notices Larissa and Mimi make their entrance. Joe has found out Chandler Murphy is being schmoozed by

Booker and Larissa who are trying to finagle a deal for a southern restaurant at the Retro. They've been trying to utilize Chandler for her culinary expertise and her in-laws prestige.

Larissa has that Foxy Brown (Pam Grier not the rapper) body and looks like a young Tina Marie with a permanent tan; she's wearing 4" Steve Madden street walkers and a sky blue halter jumpsuit. Mimi has that Holly Robinson Peete look of innocence and is toned like Angela Bassett was for her role as Tina Turner; she is wearing a light natural denim tube top style mini dress. Larissa scans the room ignoring all the attention they are getting while Mimi greets several people. Larissa locks eyes on A.J. and Phenom dancing and appears upset at what she sees. Phenom is cheering A.J. on attempting to embarrass her but she loves to dance and pays him no mind. He dances around A.J. and is moving up close on her. A.J. for a few seconds likes what she feels then gracefully moves away.

Larissa started to cross the dance floor, but not before dismissing several men on her way. A.J. notices a heated exchange between her and Booker, at one point he has a grip on her wrist and she yanks her arm from his grip. She struts over to Phenom starts dancing and asked "Mind if I cut in?" he gives her an exasperated look and replies "I'll get you later I need to check on some things" and walks away.

Beamer joins A.J. and they both watch Larissa watching Phenom walk away, obviously unhappy.

"Don't I know you?" she says to Beamer ignoring A.J. "Don't tell me, your Bianca the model, you were my idol when I was growing up", she says snidely.

"Really, so what is it you've grown up to be?"

"Oh, I tried modeling but you know, to much hips and to many lesbians. Not that I have anything against them, but I like keeping my options open;" she said while winking at A.J. who rolls her eyes and walks away.

"She's not very friendly is she?"

"Do you know her?"

"No, just a bad vibe I'm getting." Beamer shakes her head and starts to walk away, but Larissa grabs her hand and says seductively licking her lips, "I'm in room 328 if you have time to give some beauty tips."

Beamer momentarily recalls how Larissa had her girlfriend howling on tape.

"You don't need any tips from me. You and your girlfriend, looking towards Mimi, do have a goodnight."

The party goes on until the wee hours and everyone had a great time. The gift bags are over the top they contain iPods, designer sunglasses, D'Esse Spa gift certificates, and Calvin Klein Summer perfume, Tommy Boy cologne and personal DVD players. The ladies dance with several men to see if they could get any information as to how his employees felt about Phenom and they love working a room. As the ladies prepare to leave they agree that the party was fabulous.

"Excuse me miss, may I have this dance?"

Beamer turns around to see Mikel leaning on one of the decorative pillars. He is wearing all black a diamond 2 carat stud sparkled through his hair.

"Oh, she says disappointingly, my feet are killing me."

A.J. pinches her on her butt. Beamer flinches.

"That's all right I'm more formally trained when it comes to dancing, but I give an excellent foot massage."

"Goodnight" A.J. says waving her hand over her head walking away. They completely forgot she was there.

"Really?" Beamer asks in a sexy show me voice.

"Come I'll show you", he says extending his hand out to her.

She takes it. He led her out of the lobby to his car illegally parked in front.

"Are you cold?" he asks looking into her

eyes, running his index finger across her protruding nipple.

"No, I'm quite warm actually."

He grins at her and opens the car door for her. Suddenly she is swept into his arms. He takes his time with the kiss, yet there is a hunger that they both recognize.

They drive in silence to a small cottage behind an estate in Old Saybrook. Mikel ran his fingers through her hair with his free hand while he drove. Stopped at a red light he pulled her to him and kissed her with such passion that she was sure her panties were soaked. She forgot, however, that she wasn't wearing any. Rick James and Tina Maries “Fire and Desire” was playing on the radio.

When they reach their destination he opened the car door for her; kissed her gently took her hand and led her to the door.

The cottage was white with green trim a smaller version of the main house. The living area was decorated in earth tones with a rust leather sofa and love seat. The walls were painted apple green and several wooden carved art pieces adorned the walls.

"Make your self at home" he says kicking off his shoes and unbuttoning his shirt. As he walked past Beamer he pulled the string of her wrap jumpsuit loose exposing one breast.

He disappears, Beamer hears water running

she follows the sound and enters a room with a huge cat paw tub built for two. He was lighting the candles on a candelabra and the moon glowed through the glass ceiling where the stars reminded her of a night in the Dominican Republic; sparkling like jewels. He has taken off his shirt and was adding scented oils to the water.

She is still looking up in awe as he comes up behind her kisses her neck and pulls her jumpsuit down. “Somewhere There’s a Love Just for Me” starts playing.

"Let's get you in the water" he says helping her step out of her jumpsuit and into the tub. He makes no comment as to her being naked beneath her clothes.

"Aah, this feels great" she says.

He lifts her foot out of the water and starts to massage one then the other she closes her eyes and enjoys it.

"I like your style,” he says, “you are not afraid of what you want, don't want to play any coy childish games."

"I am a grown ass woman, a GAW if you will. What’s wrong with two consenting adults enjoying themselves? It can be so easy but we make it hard. We’re not in love so we can't make love, we can help each other relieve what's inside of us. I don't make it a habit of doing something like this but, I feel completely comfortable with you. Most men think its all about how I look, that's boring. I need mental stimulation and we would be foolish to let our obvious mutual attraction be a memory and it doesn't hurt that you know Joe."

"Spoken like a woman who's a realist."

"Yeah well, we're talking too much now if you ask me."

Mikel stands up and unbuttons his pants. His erection is straining through his silk boxer briefs.

"Do you have protection?"

Mikel takes a condom off one of the shelves.

"Confident, huh". Beamer says with a smirk.

"No hopeful and now grateful."

Beamer takes the condom likes that it is large and says, "Mmm strawberry."

She rolls it on and then gets on her knees and starts to lick it. She then starts to suck him, making popping noises. Mikel is groaning piling her hair up softly stroking her face and watching her with adoration.

He pulls her to her feet and turns her around and bends her over, "I must taste you" he says. Mikel gently strokes her ass wiping away the bubbly suds and spreads her ass cheeks, he runs his hands through her slit and inserts two fingers inside of her. She gasps.

He works his magic for a moment then proceeds to give her a thorough tongue lashing.

"Yes, Oh shit yeah," she says and starts to ride his face.

Beamer looks back at him and catches a glimpse of him watching her as she runs her fingers through his hair and coaches him on.

"Yes baby, right there, Oh I'm gonna cum." He moans and works her harder. She yelps and starts to shake and cums.

Mikel stands up and slips into her as she is still trembling. They move furiously then suddenly he slips out of her.

"Don't stop" she whines. He turns her around to face him, takes her face in his hands and kisses her deeply. Joining her in the tub he motions for her to mount him. She does so as a sigh of relief escapes her. Water is splashing everywhere as they kiss and do a slow grind. Mikel breaks the kiss and takes her nipple in his mouth, as she yelps again. His eyes never leave her.

"Yes baby, ride me."

And she does until they sound like two animals mating. Beamer literally sees stars with her head thrown back and she cums again. He thrust harder and roars as they cum together still rocking until both are spent.

Beamer falls on his chest and he pulls her close kisses her brow and strokes her back.

Breathing heavily they both manage to say, "Wow".

"You okay?" he asked.

All she can manage is "Meow".

They both share a laugh. He turns on the hot water with his foot and stirs the water. They recover while soaking in silence. Beamer takes notice that he is very touchy-feely.

"Let's get you to bed", he says while gently lifting her as they both hold on to stand. Mikel rises out of the tub and helps her out. He pulls her close, running his hands over her body; "you are truly beautiful", he said as he took an oversized towel and dried her and then himself. He carries her to the bedroom decorated in all mahogany oak, where one wall was a huge mirrored sliding closet.

Beamer stretched and admired herself in the mirror and catches his reflection watching her.

Stephanie Mills "Comfort of a Man" plays softly as he has turned down the volume.

"I sleep "au natural. Do you need something to sleep in?" he asks, his dick was getting hard again and he absentmindedly stroked it, still watching her.

"Who said anything about sleep" she said touching herself.

He takes a condom out of the nightstand and climbs into bed behind her and enters her.

They are facing the mirror. Her lips part but no sound escapes, she is hypnotized watching as he lifts her leg and watches himself move in and out of her. He starts to kiss her neck remembering the response he got out of her earlier by kissing her there. She turns to meet his lips and it's awkward, he rolls her over and enters her again propping her legs on his elbows.

Their eyes lock again. Beamer starts to moan and clutches his back and has a small orgasm. Mikel kisses her deeply as her body trembles slightly. They do a slow dance for several minutes reveling in their new found ecstasy. Beamer doesn't want it to end; she groans "Oh, this is sooooo, good" and cums. Mikel kisses her neck and lightly bites her nipple; she trembles. He lowers her legs. They are chest to chest as he moves her hair out of her face and strokes it.

"That was the most beautiful thing I ever saw" he said. He holds her tightly and grinds her hips deeper and harder. He makes a guttural sound while urging her to cum with him and she does.

Beamer thinks this man could break my heart. As if reading her mind he lowers himself gently on her kissing her softly, "You my goddess are a heartbreaker."

"You don't even know me" she says looking

deep into his eyes caressing his shoulders.

"Yes, I do, we were meant to meet. I saw a flicker of uncertainty in your eyes just now. You know what you want, your not afraid of letting go of yourself when it feels right. Your passion is real. Joe's told me you ended an engagement and that if I hurt you he would break both my legs." He slips out of her and she pokes out her lip.

"You are so animated," he says and laughed. "Will you runaway with me?"

"Tell me more about my eyes", a famous Bugs Bunny line, she says batting her lashes.

"What a great sense of humor" he says and roars with laughter.

"So what do you want a fuck buddy? she asks while shivering a little as he rolls off of her.

"Oh my god, forgive me, I think the fires gone out." He gets out of the bed and pulls the covers UP for her to get under and kisses her on the forehead. He then grabs a robe and goes to tend to the fire.

Beamer watches him and sighs.

Mikel returns to the bed with a glass of water for her. He disrobes and climbs in bed behind her. They cuddle as he rubs her thighs and arms.

"You warm enough? I have a down blanket I can get out of the closet?"

"No, you'll do just fine" she says and drinks half the glass of water and puts it on the night stand. "Thank you."

"As for me looking for a fuck buddy, yes that would be nice, but I'm looking for someone to fall in love with and make love to. I do not wish to scare you away, but I just thought you should know."

"I appreciate your honesty I also like to be in love and truly make love but, we need to go real slow here."

"Okay, but I warn you I may be half way there" he kisses her deeply and with passion.

"We'll talk when all of this madness is over."

"Goodnight princess", he says kissing her shoulder.

"Goodnight sir" Beamer says in her southern belle voice.

Long after Beamer hears his gentle snore and his warm breath on her back, she lie awake wondering what the hell just happened and thought of the Judge.

13

A.J. and Beamer plan to meet with Phenom, Larissa and MiMi at 5pm in his suite. The hotel rooms were covered for an additional night for those who needed to recover, at least for the Smith & Watson employees. Larissa's behavior last night made her more suspect and Beamer couldn't wait to get at that trick.

A.J. manages to get to bed around 4:30am with her hand between her legs thinking about how much fun she and Stephen had but Phenom's face kept distracting her from her goal. She finally fell asleep tired from frustration. A.J. awoke at 1 pm and decided to take advantage of the Retro's spectacular heated Olympic pool. She gets a small thrill at the sight of the pool shaped like a lima bean with psychedelic tiles. Steam is rising off the water as A.J. descends the stairs into about 3 feet of water. An "Aah" escapes her lips as she turns on her back and floats for a few seconds then turns and does about six laps. Suddenly she gets a cramp in her right calf and is struggling to get to at least the 5 feet area. "What's that smell?" she thinks. Out of nowhere Phenom emerges. Huh, where in the hell did he come from? He gently puts his arm around her waist and helps her to the stairs. Once she is sitting he gently takes her leg and she flinches.

"Relax, the more you resist the tighter it gets."

He starts to slowly caress her calf and lower thigh; his expert touch surprises her.

What is that smell? This boy is bad news. A.J. has a cousin named Ray-Ray. Who doesn't have or know someone named Ray-Ray; her cousin is often in and out of the system and every time she sees him it stinks.

A.J. refuses to make eye contact. All she can say is "Do you smell something?"

"Excuse me?"

"Forget it, it's me, look that's great" she said. Actually she's thinking to herself, “it feels fucking great”!

"You know in some cultures that would mean you owe me."

"Oh, please, it was not that serious. I’m indebted to you? Consider our taking your case making us even."

"But I'm paying you", he said smiling.

A.J. never noticed what beautiful teeth he had and such kissable lips. She could definitely see his lips on her lips and not the ones on her face. HUH!! I’m trippin she says to herself.

"You damn straight" A.J. said getting up a little unsteady. He takes her elbow, and helps her from the pool. "You’re lucky we even took your case." A.J. sat on one of the psychedelic lounge chairs, rubbed her calf, looked squarely at him and asked "What do you want?"

"How about dinner?" he asked emerging from the water like a black Adonis.

Huh? Who thought that! A.J couldn't help for doing a complete head to toe scan. Chirp!

"You mean to tell me you didn't feel some type of vibe when we were dancing last night?"

"Don't trip, it was just a dance!" she lied. Recalling when he was dancing behind her his hard dick had her bird whistling dixie.

"Okay so, how about lunch?"

"Thanks, but I don't get involved with clients. Liar, a voice says in her head. I'm also expecting room service in a few and I'm serious about not owing you."

"I know, I was just messing with you."

"Just so were on the same page. I'll see you at 5'oclock" said A.J. She then tried to be cute with her walk, knowing his eyes were crawling all over her. Yikes!

She ran into Beamer in the lobby.

"What happened to your leg?" Beamer asked.

"Forget about my leg, please tell me the masked man eats like it's his last meal."

"Girl, I'm going to be wet for days rewinding flashbacks of this one".

"Wow, so long as that tasty morsel didn't disappoint. If I find out otherwise, I'll have to arrange for him to be shot at high noon in the town square."

"He's beyond my fantasy. If he asked, I would have done just about anything he wanted last night."

"You get yours?" A.J. whispers as they get into the elevator.

"Girl I came like an avalanche. I was so wet on the way there I was embarrassed that I may have soiled his seat, especially when I remembered I wasn't wearing any underwear. But what really turned me on was that penetrating stare. It was as if he could read my mind" she whispers.

"Like Count Dracula" A.J. said.

"Wow" the say in unison.

"Yeah, he's definitely a keeper and a heartbreaker."

"Would that be Count Dracula the Prince of Darkness or the Count on Sesame Street?" A.J. asks.

"Screw you."

"Too late" they both laugh.

14

A.J., Beamer and Joe are in Phenom's suite when Larissa and Mimi arrive. They think it's a meeting. Larissa is excited as she hasn't been included in much lately especially after her brief affair ended; she took it badly. Phenom saw her for the gold digger she is and told Mimi to keep her from nagging him. When Larissa saw who was in attendance she headed straight for Phenom and gave him a hug. He took her arms from around him and said, "Let me show y'all something", and picked up the remote on the living room table and hit play.

"Who in the fuck idea was this?" He said looking at Larissa in a accusatory fashion and then at Mimi.

Mimi gasped and put her hand over her mouth.

It's the scene where Larissa is giving Davis a blow job and Mimi is watching. Phenom had to fast forward the tape to this point so as not to further embarrass his sister.

"Where did you get that?" Larissa yelled. She then snatched the remote from Phenom and stopped the show.

"Uh Oh, looks like somebody is busted" said Joe.

"This is an example of keeping your options open?

"Shut the fuck up! Who in the fuck are you, anyway?"

"You know about this shit?" Mimi says yelling at Larissa.

"I never intended to use it. After Davis died, I just put it away."

"What were you planning to do? Blackmail him?" Mimi said.

"Well, that doesn't matter much now because; someone is now trying to blackmail me. And if it wasn't for the fact that my sister is on this shit, I wouldn't give a fuck" Phenom says.

"How could you do this to me!" Mimi yells at Larissa, and then turns to Phenom, "We were high on X it was my first and last time doing that shit" she glares at Larissa then lunges at her pulling her hair. "I could kill you!"

Joe and A.J. pull Mimi off of Larissa who doesn't put up a fight. She is holding her head, maybe from the pain or the situation.

"I never would have used this against Davis. I know how close you two were, Larissa says looking at Phenom, it was just for fun."

"Where did you keep it? Did you tell anyone about it?" Beamer asks.

"In a locked box in the back of my entertainment center. I don't remember telling anyone in regular conversation." Then she sheepishly adds, "although, I may have referred to it to a few people", not making eye contact and wringing her hands.

"Like who?" asked Phenom and Mimi say at the simultaneously.

"I don't know, maybe Vladimir Crazsnow (a hockey player), Keyshawn and maybe my brother."

"This is fucking great, all of my supposed boys" Phenom said.

"Have any of them been in your apartment? Joe asks.

Larissa doesn't answer and is, wringing her hands harder.

"Have they!" A.J. yells.

"Yes. All of them."

The ringing of the room phone interrupts and Phenom answers it. "No, I am not expecting any packages. Does it say who it's from? Okay, have someone bring it up please. Thanks." A box was left at the front desk addressed to me, no return address."

15

The blackmailers had left a box at the front desk for Phenom with a note.

BRING $250,000 TO DUCK POND AT MYSTIC, SHOPPING VILLAGE AT 1pm TOMORROW. COME ALONE SLICK AND NO POLICE. WEAR THE HEAD. PRESS TALK ON THE CALL PHONE ONLY AFTER THE MONEY HAS BEEN DELIVERED TO GET THE LOCATION OF THE ORIGINAL TAPE. CNN WILL GET THE TAPE IF YOU DO NOT FOLLOW OUR INSTRUCTIONS.

Along with the note was the head of a jackass and a cell phone. Phenom refused to wear the head but Beamer and A.J. convinced him to. It was important that they go along with the demands. They were also pissed these people were not only extorting a client but now trying to make an ass, pardon the pun, of him. Somebody was going down. Phenom didn't look out of place there because the adjacent parking lot was where the parade ended and there were all kinds of characters wandering about. The money drop was to be in Ye Olde Shopping Village at Duck Tales Pond, in Mystic, CT at 1pm.

Unfortunately, it was a holiday Monday and a fuckin parade was going on. The parade was coming down Greenville Avenue and ending in the parking lot of the shopping village. Brock would be posted by the Tourism office, Charo sitting outside of the Pepsi & Dough store sampling while Beamer and A.J. would be pretending to shop. All would be in some sort of disguise in case they were recognized from the night before. The team discussed this before leaving the hotel. They were mainly concerned about the crowds of people. The Annual Week long celebration of The Great Outdoors was going on and access to vehicles would be restricted once the parade was in procession. It was going to make things tricky.

The local high school marching band was quite impressive.

"Everybody's got soul these days, huh." A.J. said smirking.

"Think they got soul; MTV has ruined the white All-American youth" Beamer replied.

"Here he comes" A.J.says and they bust out laughing.

The crowd is growing dense and it's now 1:45pm. Phenom has now started to pace in the jackass head and some kids start to taunt him. He must have said something threatening because they ran away like a thief with stolen goods. Suddenly three characters dressed as Underdog,

Courageous Cat and Mighty Mouse approach him. They converse for a minute and Phemon hands over the bag but not before tugging at it and one of the straps break, the fool in the Courageous Cat suit knees him in the balls and he goes down and the Three Stooges take off.

Brock starts doing a speed walk and Charo is on her feet already heading towards them and Underdog stops to say something admiring to her. She's just got it like that. He sees Brock running, now and panics and yells to his cohorts "Go! Go! Go!

Courageous Cat then takes off past the Liberty Bank and vaults over the bushes outside of Munsons Chocolate into Duck Pond with Beamer on his heels. "Shit!" she yells as she goes into pond. A.J. had just brought an ice cream cone and had to dump it. And just as she was about to take chase she hears a voice ask "You come hear often?" she looked around into the face of a clown, shouts "YIKES", and bolts like a mad woman.

She spots Beamer running out of the Gray Goose shop and heard the shopkeeper and customers shriek. Brock is on the heels of Underdog and Mighty Mouse who are racing towards the parking lot. Charo is helping Phenom out, while A.J. and Beamer continue to chase Courageous Cat who has run through into the Penguin, Otters and Others shop and through the Franklin General Store into the parking lot where Underdog and Mighty Mouse have jacked a hot air balloon. The hot air balloon operator is shrieking like a girl.

“Stop you long eared varmints” Beamer shouts.”

As they all head towards the balloon Brock grabs the dangling strap and yanks the bag with all his might as Courageous Cat dives into the ascending balloon. The bag hit the ground and money started to fly around. A.J. and Beamer manage to contain the situation before it turned into a feeding frenzy. Underdog is now yelling at Courageous Cat and bopping him upside the head. The balloon operator is frozen with fear.

A.J., Beamer, Brock, Maria and Phenom and a host of others watch as the balloon takes off.

“Can you believe this bullshit?” Brock said with hands on his knees trying to catch his breath.

“Jacking a hot air balloon?” “No, I don’t put shit past desperate people they’ll resort to anything” A.J. said.

“Who the fuck do they think they are desecrating the reputation of some of our greatest cartoon superheroes?” Beamer says.

“Not only that, they were all wearing your new sneaker” A.J. says to Phenom.

"What a stupid crook story" Charo says.

"We need to talk to your sister and her girl now!" A.J. says.

16

Back at the hotel they meet up with Mikel and Rashaad in Phenom's suite. He is calling his sister.

"I don't give a fuck if you ain't talking to her, you tell her to get her ass up here now!" He throws his cell phone at the sofa and starts to pace.

"Phone activity shows Larissa made several calls to several men after she left here. Probably an attempt to try and find out if one of them took the disc" Rashaad says unfolding a spreadsheet from his briefcase. Mikel and Joe walk over to look at it.

"Who were they to? Mikel asks.

"John Donaldson, Keyshawn and Booker" Rashaad says.

"John Donaldson is John Dough and she's been involved with all of them" Phenom said.

"Where's the bar in this joint?" Bruno asked.

Phenom picks up a remote and presses a button and a wall panel opens to reveal a fully stocked bar.

"Now that's what's up! Charo says.

"Bee-Bee how about a Martini? Bruno asks Beamer.

"After that episode of high-jinx today, make it a double" Beamer says.

"I'll have one too if you don't mind" Mikel said looking at Beamer slowly licking his lips.

Beamer's bird chirped.

There's a knock on the door and when Phenom opens the door Larissa rushes in and announces, "I was robbed!"

"What the fuck are you talking about?" Phenom said.

"Wait, let her finish, Mikel says. When were you robbed?"

"Last month, my apartment was broken into."

"What was taken?" asked Beamer.

"Um, Um, some jewelry, CD's, my laptop, small stuff. Mostly my place was trashed. The police thought they might have been looking for money."

"And you never thought about checking to see of the disc was gone? Joe asked.

"No, she says, looking at Phenom, I was just keeping it for myself."

"Yeah, I bet" Phenom said.

"I wasn't going to do anything with it, I kind of liked him, he was sweet" she said coyly.

"Oh, brother!" Phenom said aloud.

"Spoken like a true bubble head" A.J. says through her teeth to Beamer.

"Let's think about what our plan should be

since the first went badly, they will be pissed and watching more carefully" Joe said.

"Shouldn't we call on the phone they left?" Phenom asks.

"NO"! Mikel and Beamer say simultaneously, Mikel nod his head as if to let her speak.

"Let's wait them out. That will be where they fuck up, maybe we can trace the number" Beamer says.

"We can't it's one of those Wal-mart pay as you go phones" said Joe.

"First, can I talk to you for a moment, everybody have a drink and brainstorm or something" A.J. says walking past Phenom into his bedroom.

Phenom followed like a disobedient child.

When she's out of earshot Beamer says real ghetto like, neck twirling and all "You ain't the boss of me" evoking a laugh out of the group.

When the door was closed "You have got to calm down, we are going to meet with these fools again and they are mad and desperate, luckily no one got hurt today, this time will be tricky."

"I can't believe that b ..., I don't believe this shit, he say walking over to the window looking out at spectacular view of the wooded horizon.

"Look I need for you to focus so we can

catch these motherfuckers" A.J. said.

"Whoa! Sounds like you need to calm down; I didn't know you could cuss like that."

"Why not you know where I'm from and I'm havin serious problems with the desecration of the cartoo characters."

"What's with you and the old school cartoons?"

"I don't have time to explain that, you gotta really know me to get it, I think it's a generation thing."

"I tried to get to know, but you got these rules" Phenom says moving towards her.

He's all up in her personal space they stare like a lion and a lioness the air is thick with tension.

Feeling cocky, she moves a step closer and feels his breath on her face, "keep it up little boy, I'll be picking my teeth with your bones" she says to herself grinning and then imagines Bugs Bunny giving her good swift kick in the ass.

A knock on the door interrupts them and who else but Beamer sticks her head in, "We need you partner" she says.

"She's got great timing" Phenom says finally looking relaxed.

"Part of being a good bitch and I mean that in the most endearing way" A.J. said leaving the room.

"So what's the plan?" A.J. says ask excepting a drink from Bruno.

"We wait them out; I think a few of us should stick with Mr. Phenom in case they call. We don't want you running off by yourself dealing with these jackasses" Mikel says.

"Wait them out? What kind of plan is that?" Phenom asked.

"Let's face it we can't be dealing with rocket scientist here and we've done this enough to know they are desperate, so you can call the shots" Joe said.

"Just tell them some of the money was lost and you need time to recount and replace it, get the location for the drop and that will give us time to make our move" says Rashaad.

"We all need to eat something and rest up for now. They know you had some help and are pissed. This time they will insist upon you making the drop alone" A.J. said.

"I'll have the kitchen bring us up something and there are a couple of bedrooms through there" Phenom says pointing down a hallway.

"Mikel you take the bed I'll chill here" Joe says lying on a yellow chaise.

"I'm going to run and take a quick shower and get out of these wet nasty sneakers, then to A.J. and Bruno, you two save me something to eat" Beamer says.

Charo has turned on the television and a breaking news story is reporting "Hey, hold up look at this bullshit" she says turning the volume up.

The reporter is saying "An out of control hot air balloon has landed in the parking lot of Kids World in Brooklyn, CT, the children apparently thought it was part of the amusement at the park, but reports are coming in that the hot air balloon was skyjacked, if we can say that from a parade in Mystic, CT". In the foreground you see Mighty Mouse, Courageous Cat and Underdog running from a bunch of kids.

Everyone is dying laughing.

"I'll see if I can get in touch with the locals up there" Mikel says, I need to make some calls."

He and Beamer leave the room at the same time, in the hall they don't speak as he pushes the private elevator button. The doors open and she pressed the button for the 9th floor he doesn't press anything as the doors close. He is standing so close behind her that she feels this body heat. He moves close enough for her to feel his erection on her behind, "You see what you do to me?" he says and puts his hands down the front of her pants and finds her moist. Beamer moans and opens her legs slightly to welcome him. "Yes, princess cum for me" he says as he presses the stop button at the 19th floor on the elevator and moves in front of her pinning her against the wall.

Looking deep into her eyes puts his index and middle fingers into her and massages her clit with his thumb sucking her lip and watching her moan. She humps against his hand while holding onto his muscular arms looking back at him. She starts breathing heavy and begins to tremble. "Yes, yes let me see it". Beamer tries to stifle her moans as her knees get weak and her legs shake. He kisses her deeply as she cums, he's taking her breath while she moans into his mouth. He takes his hand out and smells it then licks it. He presses the go button on the elevator then the 12th floor button. He holds her tightly until the elevator stops at his floor he kisses her forehead and gets off.

"Tonight?" he asks.

She just looks at him and shakes her head. As the door closes he walks away and she hears a low sinister, Vincent Price type laugh.

Beamer slinks to the floor and when the elevator opens on the 9th floor and a maid is standing there.

"Lord I've fallen in lust with the devil" she says out loud.

"Que? Are you alright senorita?"

"Did anyone get the number of that bus?"

17

Joe, Brock and Phenom are watching Monday Night Football when the phone left by the blackmailers rings. Joe jumps up to activate the tracking device the screen shows "Unknown Name, Unknown Number."

"Fuck!" Brock shouts to the others.

Beamer, A.J., Charo and Mikel come from the game room, they were playing pool.

"Okay pick it up" Mikel tells Phenom.

Those bozos are using a voice disguise apparatus that sounds like Mickey Mouse, Joe has it on speaker for everyone to hear. "Who do you think you're fucking with slick? You and your little security people think their clever? That's gonna cost you $100,000 more. No more games, you come alone and if we spot any police the deal is off."

"I need more time all of the money isn't here". Phenom says.

"Then get it motherfucker!!

"You saw what happened in the parking lot, I haven't even recounted it yet" Phenom says in a pleading tone.

"Um, hold on" the voice says.

Joe shakes his head "This is what we want them flustered" he says in almost a whisper.

"Okay jackass, the voice says tauntingly, bring all of the money to the Ocean Beach Park at 1:00 tomorrow, go to the last stall in the mens room leave the money there when we get the money you will get the disc."

The line goes dead.

"You get anything?" Beamer asks.

"No, damn it!, I knew we wouldn't but we needed to try" Joe responds.

"We don't have enough time to get a warrant for phone company records and since they've scratched out the serial number it's kind of futile" Mikel says.

"Maybe we should just give them the money and stop all this cops and robbers drama" Phenom says sounding defeated.

"Let me tell you something this is the beginning of your worst nightmare especially if you start paying these jackasses off. I've seen it, it won't stop until your broke or you do something so stupid you'll wind up hurting yourself or in prison, I can't believe you gonna cave just like that" A.J. says.

"Si popi, especially after they made you wear that jackass suit" Charo says.

"You seem like a stand up guy and I've been a lawyer a long time she's right it won't end. You'll get so fucking pissed off and frustrated at being under someone's thumb at their beck and call, you'll become a regular patsy to them til you snap" Brock says.

"It's your dime you tell us what you want to do" Beamer says, A.J. gives her a look knowing they are working him.

"Look let's not bullshit a bullshitter, we think this whole thing is fucked up and want these guys to pay for what they're trying to do to you. The fact that this is someone you probably know and let in your circle they deserve to be held accountable for their actions" says Mikel who has been on the phone.

"Okay, what yaw'll wanna do?" Phenom asks.

"Joe and I are supposed to ride in the Bikers for Children's Charity Ride this Saturday. Who here can ride?

Everyone but Rashaad raises his or her hand.

"Oh that's fuckin handicap discrimination" Rashaad says jokingly.

"I can get us some loaner bikes. The beach is open to the public so we can act under the guise of a group of bikers meeting at the beach" Joe says.

"Then what"? asks A.J.

"Then we take these mofo's down" says Brock.

"Alrighty then, let's get some shut eye and be ready to ride at noon" Joe says.

18

Ocean Beach Park located in New London, CT across from the Long Island Sound provides a the ideal family beach experience that includes a boardwalk, water slide, arcade, outdoor pool, the Mullenville International Slot Car Raceway, playscape and carousel. Between 1890 and 1930, 600 carousels were made in the USA, several of the remaining 200 are scattered throughout the New England area. Beamer and A.J. still love to ride them.

The beach was busy with activity as the team arrived on bike with their helmets on to disguise themselves several minutes behind Phenom who road in a rental car. The limousine he arrived in Connecticut just wouldn't do. Rashaad followed him into the mens room acting as a civilian and wearing his prosthetic arm since he was not at Duck Pond and hopefully would not be recognized from the party. Rashaad has a black belt in karate and will chop anyone down like a tree.

The last stall has an Out of Order sign on the door, when Phenom tries it, the door opens. Outside the team watches as a midget come by and places a "Closed for Cleaning" sign outside the mens room. A.J. lured him into her web by flirting with him and asking if he worked there and he told her some guy dressed like a clam paid him to do it saying he was setting his brother up for a prank.

"They want to make sure no one gets the bag before they do" A.J. says to Bruno.

The team is wired for sound to hear and talk to one another.

"He's in the stall next to me, I don't hear anyone else, I'm going to stand on the seat and see what I can."

Looking over the stall he sees Phenom reading a note. Phenom looks up to see Rashaad and is startled.

"Yo, what's up with that? I could have been taking a piss."

"Relax, what does it say?" Rashaad say in almost a whisper.

There is someone still in one stall but the "Closed for Cleaning" sign cut down traffic for a few minutes.

"Leave the bag and go back to the hotel and wait for instructions" Phenom reads.

"Okay, you leave and we'll take care of the rest."

Phenom put the bag down and leaves.

The Seafood Midday March is lining up to begins its procession up Ocean Avenue to Bank Street towards Governor Winthrop Boulevard ending at Eugene O'Neill Drive to entertain the cities workers and ends at 3:00pm.

Phenom walks out of the mens room around the "Closed for Cleaning" sign and walks to his rental car heading out just before the procession.

A couple of characters dressed as a Shrimp with a baby shrimp strapped to his back and a Fish Stick with what is supposed to be a dollop of tartar sauce on top approach. The Shrimp enters the mens room as Fish Stick stands outside trying to look normal but acting as a look out.

"This may be them Rashaad, look alive" Joe said.

Rashaad flushes the toilet, goes to sink to wash his hands and he acts like he's having a hard time with the soap dispenser and washing his good hand. The Shrimp enters the "Out of Order" stall, looks around and shakes his head at Rashaad as he enters. Rashaad hears the bag being unzipped and zipped. Rashaad then pretends to be fighting with the paper towel dispenser as The Shrimp passes.

"The Shrimp is on the move with the bag" he says into his mike.

"Alright everybody, stay with them" A.J. says as the team starts up their bikes. With her helmet still on she then acts like she's going to the restroom when she sees them disappear from sight.

The Shrimp and the Fish Stick go behind the restroom building to a secluded area and take the miniature size stuffed shrimp and rips out it innards and stuff the money bag inside. The Fish Stick makes an attempt to cover him but A.J. manages to spot them as she stoops to fake tying her shoe near a hot dog vendor.

"They're heading towards the parking lot A.J. says.

All of a sudden Phenom's car comes careening straight towards them and jumps the sidewalk and crashes into the Boardwalk.

"What the fuck was he trying to do? Kill them?" Mikel asks.

The Shrimp and the Fish Stick start running weaving through the marching band which is playing "Under the Sea", towards the Mermaid float jump aboard and have a laugh.

The team takes off after them as Rashaad

and Charo run to see about Phenom.

Beamer, Joe, Mikel, Brock and A.J. all head toward the float. A.J. is riding with Joe and says "Let's follow them from here. They probably think Phenom snapped and Rashaad and Charo are good Samaritans helping out."

"Look at those assholes laughing like that shit is funny. I've had just about enough of these games, let's get this shit over with" Beamer says.

The Shrimp and the Fish Stick are riding on the side of the float, holding on with one hand like firemen, waving at the small crowd, reveling in their success.

"I have an idea, A.J. says, Bruno get close to them I'm going to swipe the baby and pass the bag to Beamer. Joe you and Mikel ride up ahead of the float and jump them after we take off."

"Let's do this", Joe says to Mikel.

The procession hasn't picked up its marching tempo and is proceeding slowly up Bank Street.

The Shrimp is enjoying his fifteen minutes of fame and is really getting into waving at the crowd, with his back to the street he doesn't even notice them when A.J. and Brock speed by snatch the baby shrimp off his back. The Shrimp topples over but manages to land on his feet into the path the Cycling Guppies. The Fish Stick notices his partner in traffic and the Shrimp is trying to act out to him that the money bag was snatched. The Shrimp waves through the procession of Dancing Crabs and back through the Cycling Guppies and yanks the Fish Stick off the float.

Beamer watches and reports to the team. "They're headed towards you A.J., slow up and let them think they're getting close" she says.

A.J. and Brock pretend to be slowed by the King Neptune float. Mikel and Joe have parked their bikes by the Greyhound station and run up behind the culprits.

"My cuffs won't fit them, what are we going to use?"

Joe pulls a blade out of nowhere and cuts the tassels off of the tuba player's shoulders and throws one to Mikel. Joe's movements were so fluent and swift that no one noticed, not even the tuba player.

The Shrimp and the Fish Stick are frantically trying to get to A.J. and Brock doesn't notice Joe and Mikel coming up behind them. Mikel taps the Fish Stick on the shoulder and jabs him in the face so quickly he falls into Mikel's arms like a girl. Joe taps the Shrimp and put what looks like the Dr. Spock Vulcan Grip on his shoulder and the Shrimp crumbles like a house of cards.

Joe and Mikel drag them of to the side rolls them on their backs and tie their hands. A.J. and Beamer run over and A.J. pulls of the Shrimps and then the Fish Sticks heads. It was Sammy David, Jr. and some punk that was at the party with him, whose name they did not know.

Mikel starts reading them their rights to include the fact that extortion is a federal offense.

"Hey, I was just helping my cousin, I don't wannna go to jail" the Fish Stick says.

"Okay, that tells me you two geniuses didn't put this plan together? Who put you up to this crap?" A.J. says nudging him with her foot.

"Yo, watch that sister, we smarter than you think, and I ain't talkin" Sammy says.

Joe grips the wrist of the Fish Stick with his thumb and index fingers nd applies pressure, he screams.

"Okay, okay it was Spenser" he yells.

"You punk ass", the Shrimp says.

Joe applies the same hold to the Shrimp and he yells.

"Aaah, let the fuck go of me."

"Who's the punk now? Beamer asks.

"Uggh, I knew it!!!!" A.J. exclaims.

"What?" Beamer asks.

"Slick!! In both the notes Phenom was referred to as "slick". When we saw him with Keyshawn at the Retro he called Phenom "slick."

"Ooooh, I hate when I miss things like that" Beamer said bopping herself on the head.

"Don't feel bad, we both missed it. Something was nagging me and that was it."

"I have a car coming to get these two. We'll pick up Spenser. Is he still at the hotel?" Mikel says.

"No one is leaving without the great leader Evel Kenievel back there" Sammy says laughingly referring to Phenom. And Spenser ain't leaving without that money."

"I have an idea!" A.J. and Beamer say in unison.

"You thinking what I'm thinking? Beamer asked.

"I hope it's not what I'm thinking" Joe

says.

“Probably” Beamer said looking sheepishly innocent at Joe.

“Oh, hell to the naw!! He exclaims.

19

Charo rode with the ambulance to the hospital with Phenom. Back at the hotel Bruno reported that some of Phenom's entourage is checking out as scheduled. Brock spots Spenser heading for the parking garage where Sammy said they were to meet at 6pm. The third punk was Sammy's cousin Curly, he was so traumatized by the hot air balloon incident and being chased by 30 kids that he bailed out in the middle of the night.

Sammy admits that he was sleeping with Larissa who was once engaged to Spenser. Her brother Booker was jealous of Phenom's and Davis's friendship and told Sammy about the tape. Sammy was pulled over by the police several months ago after a high speed chase and charged with DWI. Spenser was called to bail Sammy out of jail. The first week of dismal album sales had Sammy acting the fool for attention and the media loved it. Phenom publicly admonished Sammy for his behavior and then Spenser privately for trying to bribe the arresting officers. The arresting officers wanted to meet and take pictures with Monei Phenomenal Records R & B singer told this bit of information to Phenom. Good Grief !!!

While drowning themselves in their sorrows at a Phenomenal Records event Sammy let it slip to Spenser that the disc existed. Several weeks later Spenser came up the extortion plan. This would explain why both had motive for plotting against Phenom and Spenser could have his revenge against Larissa for dumping him.

Rashaad pulls up to the garage with A.J. and Beamer awaiting instructions. The desk clerk after seeing his credentials informed Mikel that according to the valet records Mr. Hornsby's car was parked on Level 3. Mikel passed this information on to Beamer. Mikel then raced towards the nearest men's room with Joe.

Rashaad reaches the 3rd parking level and waits for Spenser. After about ten minutes Spenser appears and puts his bags in the trunk of a black Mercedes. He then walks around and sits on the hood of the car obviously waiting for someone.

After waiting about fifteen minutes the Fish Stick and the Shrimp appear on the approaching ramp with the original duffle bag containing the money. Spenser hops off the hood rubbing his hands together greedily laughing.

“You guys are a riot. Those get-ups are outrageous. What creative geniuses. So, I take it everything went well partner. I must leave a big tip to my guy at the costume shop for being so accommodating” he said.

The Shrimp hands Spenser the bag. Spenser turns his back to them placing the bag on the car to examine its contents. When he finds the bag stuffed with confetti paper he turns around with rage all over his face. Mikel is holding up his badge with Joe by his side holding the costume headpieces.

Holding up his hands he immediately started to stammer, “Look guys those two thugs made me do it. They threatened my family” he says in an effort to appear the victim.

“Explain it to the District Attorney” Mikel said handcuffing him and reading him his rights.

20

The next morning the entire team was outside the hotel saying their good byes. Brock is excitedly inviting Mikel to the wedding. A.J. and Beamer have decided to stay a couple of days to shop for furnishings for the New London house.

"I don't know what you guys were really doing up to here, but I hope I get a good report" a voice behind A.J. says. She turned around to see Chandler Murphy with a bellhop loading her bags into a car.

"You're not my business, but I must compliment you on the catering. The food was fantastic, very haute cuisine" A.J. said walking away. Beamer is going riding with Mikel and will meet her at the house.

A limousine pulls up in front of A.J. The window rolls down everyone looks inside, it's Phenom. He has a soft cast from his ankle to under his knee.

"Hey guys, great job" he says.
Everyone crowds around to say good-bye.

"Going my way young lady?" Phenom asks.

Everyone suddenly disappears except Beamer who whispers to A.J., while slipping the car keys out of her hand, "Go ahead girl, have some fun" quickly walking away before A.J. can protest.

A.J. looks at him and he stares back and smiled as she opens the door and climbs in across his lap.

"The Troll" sat in a filthy office in the dungeon of the Cold Case evidence locker at the 129 Precinct picking at the hairy chin mole and chewing on her unstyled dirty blond home cut hair. Her incessant flatulence problem became unbearable for her co-workers and she was banished to the dungeon a year ago. When her "best friend" left the department to start a private investigation agency "The Troll" was crushed. She tried to apply for jobs at the agency or even work part-time security in the building. But she couldn't make it through an interview without farting. Hunched over the box she took meticulous care in wrapping the surprise, her "friend" would love it.

Til the Next Episode

God is good – all the time

“For I know the plans I have for you, declares the Lord, Plans to prosper you and not to harm you, plans to give you hope and a future”

Jeremiah 29:11

"But you be strong and do not lose courage, for there is reward for your work."
-2 Chronicles 15:7

Thanks first and foremost to God for being good all the time. To my parents, in their eternal rest, Thank you for teaching me to have no doubts, fears or questions about his goodness, for he's kept me in the midst of it all. Thanks for always being there for my siblings and me, and always putting us first. My adoring husband, who has supported me emotionally and financially, thanks for letting me follow my dream and especially for pushing me. Cedra Walton my best "friend in the whole world" you started all this madness in Acapulco, with your documentary; you are truly my sister and my inspiration.
All my siblings, especially Harriet, Dexter, Gil and Junior for all your encouragement. My cousins Henrietta Walden, Phillip Douglas, Naison Johnson, Melissa Jarrett, Stanley and Dominga for always being interested and encouraging about the book.

A very special thanks to my cousins Darren & Linda Douglas, Christopher and Lourdes Douglas for allowing me to escape at their fabulous "cribs" and attain the peace I needed space to create, you have no idea how much it meant to me. All of my maternal aunts and uncles. Mr. John E. Bowe my editor, for always listening and being there. When I thought of an editor I knew it would have to be someone who "got me" and you were exactly what I book needed, I will be eternally grateful. Your direction and advice were invaluable to me completing this book and will continue to help with the series; I could not have done this without your help. Harold and Stephanie Brantley our "clone couple", whose friendship Rick and I will always treasure. Thanks to Anthony Curry and Kendrick Williams for providing their comments for my initial content feedback and their encouragement. Detective Morris “Mo” Weathers for being a true friend in all your thugishness.

Attorney-at-Law Professor Angela Burton, thanks for all your efforts. Jerry O'Donnell, for taking a chance on Rick and always looking out. The employees and fellow volunteers at Dress for Success, after my loss of my parents I needed to be around people who were truly concerned about others, a quality my mom possessed. I was revitalized in so many ways and rediscovered the true meaning of "tis better to give than to receive". You are doing God's work and will always be an inspiration to me. Rose Laface you understood what I was going through and have the biggest heart. Your loyalty will never be forgotten. Andreia Whack for her initial involvement and support, Monique Hendricks and Charmain Stephens I have always admired your loyalty to our friendship and will treasure ours always.

Rory Grady my brother-in-law for being my other husband. You are truly my brother. Stephen and Donna Punch, whenever I saw you, you always asked about the book and were enthusiastic every step of the way. All of my nieces and nephews, you bring my heart such joy and I am proud of you all. Bobby Fryer I was getting so discouraged when I found you and after a slow start you brought the vision of the characters I developed to life, I definitely see our next cover. I have been blessed with some fabulous brother and sister in laws and Thank God for bringing you to the family. Cecil Carryl you led me to an alternative for the cover and being an ear. My "Glam Squad" Stacy Pelham Hale, Harriet Hale and Lisa Darroux you guys are truly fabulous. Dr. Marvin Goldstein, Dr. William Kutcher and Dr. Mark Silverman who all saw my health improve once I stopped working, you are life savers. I am living the life meant for me.

"There but for the grace of God I go".

Hair: Stacy Pelham Hale
Photo: Harriet Hale
Makeup: Lisa Darroux

www.ingramcontent.com/pod-product-compliance
Ingram Content Group UK Ltd.
Pitfield, Milton Keynes, MK11 3LW, UK
UKHW020141250726
13967UKWH00002B/787

9 781425 121006